THE GRASS WIDOW

by
Ralph McInerny

A
FATHER DOWLING
Mystery

THE VANGUARD PRESS
NEW YORK

Library of Congress Cataloging in Publication Data

McInerny, Ralph M.
    The grass widow.

    I. Title.
PS3563.A31166G7   1983   813'.54   82-24775
ISBN 0-8149-0866-7   AACR2

Designer: Tom Torre Bevans.
Manufactured in the United States of America.
1 2 3 4 5 6 7 8 9 0

To

Nancy and Don Kommers

1

MARIE MURKIN, the housekeeper at St. Hilary's rectory in Fox River, Illinois, acted as if no other female had ever asked to see the pastor. But then this visitor simply informed Mrs. Murkin that she would see Father Dowling, as if she had made an appointment. And there was more.

Clare O'Leary was in her mid-thirties but she still wore her ash-blonde hair as long as a schoolgirl's. The camel's-hair coat, mahogany loafers, and paisley print scarf — her whole outfit, aspect, and manner — to the degree Mrs. Murkin could assess these in the minute that passed as she put the visitor in the parlor and went to inform Father Dowling of her arrival — incurred the housekeeper's disapproval.

Mrs. Murkin stood in the door of the study, darted her eyes down the hall toward the parlor, lifted them to heaven, and sighed audibly.

"Someone to see you," she said, as if Father Dowling would not have heard the front bell. "Ms. Clare O'Leary." Marie prolonged the sobriquet until it became a menacing buzz.

"Show her in here, Marie."

"She's already settled in the parlor."

If Marie Murkin had her way, the only one allowed to see what she regarded as the mess of Father Dowling's study would have been Phil Keegan, Captain of Detectives on the Fox River police force and boyhood friend of Roger Dowling. Phil Keegan counted as family. He was certainly a frequent presence in the rectory—for meals, for cribbage, for Cub games. Marie looked on the verge of mutiny at the suggestion that she go fetch the guest.

"The parlor is such a cheerless place."

"I do what I can," Mrs. Murkin said, each word a separate expression of long-suffering. Roger Dowling applied a match to his pipe. Marie went on, "Besides, not everyone enjoys living in a cloud of tobacco smoke."

"I'll see her here, Marie."

In the moment before she left, Marie had the look of St. Sebastian receiving a dozen darts at once. When she showed the woman into the study, Ms. O'Leary lifted a hand that held a lighted cigarette. "I take it you won't mind this?"

"Hardly."

"I love pipe smoke." Behind her Marie closed her eyes in pain and fled to her kitchen. "My name is Clare O'Leary." She reached her hand across the desk.

"Roger Dowling."

Before she was settled in the chair across from him she said, "Father, I've left my husband."

She exhaled smoke, her mouth slightly open, studying him. Roger Dowling had mixed memories of Tallulah Bankhead and Bette Davis. He puffed on his pipe. They might have been exchanging signals.

"I drove here, took a room in a motel, and looked up your number in the directory."

"How did you settle on me?"

"I had heard your name before."

He suppressed the desire to ask where. It would have seemed vain. It would have *been* vain. "Why have you left your husband?"

"Because he wants to kill me."

She made the incredible remark almost nonchalantly before busying herself with extinguishing her cigarette in the ashtray he pushed toward her.

"Why?"

Her smile was enigmatic. "The usual reason. Another woman. The difference is that she is an older woman. Somehow that makes it worse, I don't know why. Larry is at the age when he is supposed to try recapturing his youth with someone younger. God knows he has enough opportunity for that. But no. He has to be different. With him, it is an older woman."

"Larry O'Leary?"

"Isn't that awful? He had a father with that kind of sense of humor. Larry inherited it. Have you ever listened to him?"

"I don't understand."

"Larry O'Leary is a radio personality. He is a hot ticket on WKIS in Waukegan."

"I don't believe I have."

"You wouldn't like him. Father Hogan thinks the world of him. Do you know Davie Hogan? He knows you."

"Is he your pastor?" Roger Dowling did know Hogan, not well: he was a dim figure from the past. Ahead of him in the seminary or behind? He did not remember.

"I went to him with this. Not that he needed me to tell him. He just laughed and then told Larry I had been to see him."

"Why not go to the police?"

"With what?"

"What makes you think your husband intends to kill you?"

"Oh, it's no secret. He has announced it on the air."

"He broadcast on the radio his intention to kill you?"

She took a package of cigarettes from her bag and extracted one as she nodded. "Big joke. It's an occupational hazard, I've always known that. Everything in Larry's life is grist for the mill, something he can turn into chatter on the air. He goes through material like a plague of locusts. Nothing is private, nothing is sacred. It's become a minor motif. 'When I kill my wife' or 'Let me tell you, it's no easy matter to take out a contract on your wife. Believe me, I know. I've been trying for years.' That sort of thing passes for humor."

"Surely he's only joking."

□ 3 □

"That's what you're supposed to think. He's told me he's perfectly serious."

"That's not a very serious way to go about it. I really don't know what to tell you. You're right that the police couldn't do anything on this basis. They're reluctant to intervene in domestic disputes in any case."

"Father, even if you don't believe me, it's good to be talking to you about it."

"I haven't said I don't believe you." Nor that he believed her. For whatever reason, she had left her husband and come to him for help. Despite her surface manner, a calmness not wholly negated by the nervous smoking, Roger Dowling heard in Clare O'Leary's modulated tones a cry for help. What did she expect from him? "Maybe you're right to get away for a few days."

She shook her head. "I moved out, Father. When I left Waukegan today, it was for good."

"Did you leave some word for your husband?"

"No! The whole point was to escape."

"What are your plans?"

She considered the burning tip of her cigarette, shrugged, then looked across the desk at him. She seemed both lost and resolute. "For the moment I'm just happy I had the courage to leave him."

"Would you like some coffee?"

"Don't bother."

"It's no bother at all." He indicated the Mr. Coffee in the corner of the room. She offered to pour and he let her, pondering her remark about getting away from her husband. Perhaps that did take courage of a sort. But during his days on the Archdiocesan Marriage Court he had met many like Clare O'Leary, spouses anxious to escape their marriages, for good reasons and bad, yet once they were free of the past in one sense they found they could never be free of it in another. Let Clare O'Leary enjoy her moment of relief. Maybe she needed to think her husband was going to kill her in order to bring herself to leave.

She put a cup before Father Dowling and sat, holding her own coffee in one hand, her cigarette in the other. She looked as if she could indeed now face the world alone.

"What would your husband gain from killing you, Mrs. O'Leary?"

"Please call me Clare. He'd get rid of me. And I suppose he'd make some money from it. Insurance. Though he usually speaks of how much it will cost him to have me killed."

"Why wouldn't he simply leave you or let you go?"

"And get a divorce? Father, you don't understand Larry at all. He doesn't believe in divorce. Don't you see, he needs death to part us. Infidelity and murder are not on the same level at all: divorce is inconceivable."

"You said there was a woman."

"Yes. An older woman." That did seem to bother her. "Andrea Kohler."

"Who is she?"

"His lawyer. She draws up his contracts, makes out his income tax, advises him generally. Keeps him out of jail, is the way Larry puts it."

"How old is old?"

"Larry is thirty-seven." Her eyes drifted away. "Four years older than me. Andrea is forty-six. She is very attractive, I always knew that, but she was ten years older than Larry. Why would I worry about her? My concern was with all the breathless young things who take jobs around a station because they are gaga about anything even remotely connected with show biz. To them Larry comes across as a kind of star. And all along, the hanky-pank was with Andrea."

"How do you know?"

"Because he made no great effort to conceal it. Bills for our credit cards came to the house. Motel bills when he hadn't been on trips." Clare O'Leary looked abject. "Learning something like that is terrible for a woman. It does terrible things to you. I began to spy on Larry. The first time I saw him with Andrea I was so relieved I wanted to run up to the two of them. And then he kissed her and I stayed put in my car. Slowly one and one began to make two. Andrea! Still I refused to believe it, but whenever I followed him, there she was. They were meeting in motels at odd hours during the day. Isn't this sordid?"

"Yes."

"And there I am, following him around, spying on him. And if that isn't bad enough, he regards *me* as the trouble and says he is going to have me killed."

"Did you talk with him about Andrea?"

"No. I couldn't bring myself to talk about it. What he was doing made me feel ashamed. As if I was being unfaithful to him. That *was* a temptation." Again her eyes drifted away and Roger Dowling felt she had come to the point of her visit.

"Do you know anyone in Fox River?"

"I came here to hide."

From whom? He did not want to scare her off by asking her directly if she had been unfaithful to her husband. It would not be the first time a spouse had struck back by committing the very wrong that had been done her. Nor would it be the first time that a visitor to the rectory took the long way round to tell him what the real trouble was. If she was going to be in Fox River a few days, there was no need to force the issue now.

If Clare had come to him to speak of (and, he hoped, confess) her own transgressions, she continued now to talk of her husband's antics with Andrea Kohler and his jocular airborne threats on her life. Perhaps she was just rehearsing what she regarded as excuses for herself. If they were not going to get to the real reason she had sought out a priest, at least not on this first visit, the question arose as to what to do with Clare until he saw her again. The thought of having Mrs. Murkin look out for her came and went quickly. Marie's attitude when she brought his visitor in ruled that out. Edna Hospers, who looked after the parish center that had once been the school? Edna and Clare were approximately the same age. But Clare waved away the suggestion.

"Not on your life, Father. I intend to enjoy these first moments of freedom and by that I mean the solitude. Don't feel sorry for me sitting all alone in the motel. I am going to love every minute of it. May I come see you again?"

"I'm counting on it." How little he really knew about her. Were there any children? None had been mentioned, but parents in personal trouble can be remarkably self-centered.

Clare sat forward but did not stand. She gave him a bleak smile. "I just realized that I came to you for approval. Isn't that silly? I'm not all that different from Larry after all. I want a priestly blessing on my decision to leave him."

He let it go at that for now. Tomorrow the rectory might look inviting compared to her motel. He asked her to come see him again.

"I say Mass at noon. Before or after is fine."

He went with her to the door and watched her stride out to her car, hair tossing, the scarf hanging over her shoulder. She waved jauntily before getting into the little foreign car parked at the curb. She spun her wheels as she pulled away and then went rapidly up the street.

"Is she gone?" It was some minutes later. Marie Murkin stood in the door of the study.

"Yes."

"Where is she from?"

"She's staying right here in town."

"Where?"

For answer he gave her a look. He could not have given her much more. He had forgotten to ask Clare O'Leary what motel she was staying in.

2

PHIL KEEGAN, Captain of Detectives, sat in his office after returning from a conference with Robertson, the Chief of Police. There
were moments when Keegan understood why some men take to
drink, and this was one of them. The parallel might sound exalted,
but he wondered if the joint chiefs of staff didn't feel like this
when they reported to a civilian who was also a politician. At
least presidents were elected. Robertson was the beneficiary of
the gang that had controlled Fox River politics since before Keegan joined the department. Robertson himself had been chief only
a few years, after an undistinguished career as a cop. He had
worn the uniform five years and then taken leave to fill one of the
minor but lucrative posts his cohorts had at their disposal. His appointment as chief had cast a pall of gloom over the department
that never really lifted, only became so familiar as to be bearable.
Except to Keegan. He had to see Robertson too often to be able to
pretend the chief didn't exist. He had just spent half an hour resisting Robertson's suggestion that some of Keegan's people be
temporarily transferred to traffic.

"Do you know what we could take in in fines if we made a
real push? Of course you do."

Robertson reminded Keegan of cigarette ads in the thirties
and forties. Slicked back hair parted in the middle. His cigarette,
in the center of his mouth, bobbed up and down. The loosened
necktie suggested someone awaiting hanging, the cigarette a last

request. Wishful thinking. Robertson had the habit of conversing with himself. Keegan welcomed the eccentricity, since it made any reply from himself superfluous.

"We could double the take with a little effort."

"Easily."

"Let's do it."

"I can't spare the personnel."

"I want Lamb on traffic."

"No."

"That black woman, Agnes Lamb."

"I know who you mean. I can't spare her." Keegan recognized the clumsy hand of Peanuts Pianone. Peanuts hated blacks. What he felt for Agnes went beyond that. In a matter of months she had become ten times the cop Peanuts was. He must have talked to his relatives on the council and they in turn to Robertson.

"What's she doing?"

"Drug traffic."

Nothing in Robertson's expression changed. Keegan could believe that Robertson had convinced himself, deep in his bought-and-paid-for soul, that the drug scene in Fox River was nonexistent. He would like to see him try to prove that to Agnes Lamb.

"Drugs," Robertson repeated.

"The Harley case."

Robertson grew red. When he took the cigarette from his mouth it adhered to his lip and he had to lick it loose. "You have her working on a closed case?"

"She is after the kind of rat who has been preying on her people."

"What in God's name does that have to do with a suicide in a cheap hotel?"

Robertson might be the only person in town who accepted the suicide verdict in the Harley case. For Keegan to have proved otherwise would have taken more support than he could get from the prosecutor's office or the chief. Not that Agnes was out to rescue Harley from a suicide verdict. It was a favor to the man to imagine he had finally learned to despise himself.

It had taken Keegan twenty minutes to save Agnes Lamb from traffic duty. His suggestion that he would team Agnes and Peanuts shifted the tide. To take pleasure in such a victory seemed a measure of his current discontent. Phil Keegan loved being a cop. He dreaded retirement more than death. But he could not conceal from himself that Fox River was not a clean city. There had always been unstated limits beyond which his zeal must not carry him. Most days he could ignore this, but not when the subject was drugs and he had to confront the large accusative eyes of Agnes Lamb. He shared her desire to make the city clean as a whistle. But he had had long sad experience of indictments, trials, forgetful witnesses, and acquittals that mocked what every cop knew.

He had been five minutes back at his desk when the call from Horvath came. A woman had been found dead in a motel off I-94.

"Homicide?"

He could imagine Horvath's Slavic face, as uncommunicative as the map of eastern Europe. Cy's single expression permitted people to assign it whatever meaning they wished. It was a legend in the department that people, especially women, could not help telling all they knew to the stolid lieutenant. He was the best man Keegan had.

"The medical examiner says death is due to the bottle of sleeping tablets she swallowed."

"But you have your doubts?"

"Better come over here, Captain. This is something you'll want to take care of yourself."

It was not like Cy to be skeptical of the work of the mobile crime unit. Something was up. Keegan said he would be right over.

"Who is the woman, Cy?"

"Her name is O'Leary. Clare O'Leary."

*   *   *

The Stagecoach Inn faced Jackson Avenue and was located
midway between two intersections. Jackson, an eight-lane, concrete thoroughfare along which, night and day, whined a ceaseless
flow of traffic — semis, automobiles, service vehicles, buses, cabs,
more trucks — seemed a symbol of the price paid for technical and
industrial progress. The fumes of all those motors hung in the air
and dulled the once bright colors of the Stagecoach although its
great sign flashed greetings to passers-by. Twinkie Zeugner was
now appearing in the Billet-Doux Lounge.

Keegan waited for a break in the oncoming traffic to make a
turn into the motel. Finally he took a chance that succeeded and
bounced hard when he hit the sharp rise of the ramp. He pulled
into the spot reserved for the assistant manager. Cy stood by the
van of the mobile crime unit, waiting for him. Only a mind-reader
could have told if Horvath was glad to see him. Keegan pointed
to the motel sign.

"What's a Twinkie Zeugner?"

"A guy who plays piano. Been here for months."

"Popular demand?"

"Don't ask me."

Inside, the manager scooted from behind the reception counter and glided swiftly across the deep pile carpet to intercept them
in the middle of the lobby.

"Are you almost finished here, Lieutenant?" He must have
majored in talking while smiling in Motel Management School.

"This is Captain Keegan. William Ganser."

Keegan nodded at Ganser but the manager insisted on shaking hands. He was a man in his fifties, overweight, slack-jawed,
thin hair teased into ringlets that emphasized the fact that he was
all but bald. His glasses were of the kind that vary in tint with the
amount of light. He faced the outer door and they were growing
pink. The general impression was of a rabbit. Ganser spoke confidentially, almost in a whisper.

"Few guests have an inkling anything has happened. Of course there is a constant turnover. Plus your men have been discreet and I appreciate it. We are somewhat prepared for this sort of thing. People do die in motels. More often than you might imagine." He stopped and shook his head. Silly me. "I don't mean you gentlemen. But the public at large..."

Keegan said, "We'll do our job and get out of here. Your problem is the press, not us."

Through the open double doors of a bar off the lobby Keegan had caught a glimpse of Mervel and Ninian, Fox River's more intrepid members of the fourth estate. Ninian was a stringer for the *Trib* and Mervel wrote for the Fox River *Messenger*, which appeared six days a week and was not, as its enemies maintained, a shoppers' guide.

Ganser's eyes rolled to the ceiling stippled with fireproof concrete. "Dear God, don't I know it." When his eyes opened they went toward the bar and there was real hatred in his look.

"The staff has been helpful," Horvath said when they were walking down a seemingly endless corridor. The low ceiling made it even more claustrophobic. On the few occasions Keegan let the thought of retirement enter his head he imagined a life lived in the unreal atmosphere of motels.

The body still lay on the bed as it had been found by the maid at one-thirty that afternoon. Keegan was startled by the woman's beauty even in death. Her ash-blonde hair might have been arranged on the pillow, and the open eyes, from where Keegan stood, did not seem sightless. Phelps stood beside the bed. He was here to corroborate his assistant's finding of apparent suicide.

"Is she dead, Doc?"

The soul of caution, Phelps would emphasize "apparent" rather than "suicide." Any judgment that permitted him to jump several ways as the future required was acceptable to him. In court his testimony seldom was of much help to the prosecutor, since in murder cases Phelps could make death and not merely homicide seem alleged.

At Keegan's question, Phelps's nostrils expanded and contracted. He would not be drawn. To his lackeys in white he said, "Very well. Remove her now." Keegan and Horvath got out of the way, stepping to the wall of the room that was covered by a huge drape. Keegan found the cord and opened the drape, revealing large dirty windows that looked out on Jackson. The woman's body was zipped into the rubber bag, her hair tucked in last, and for a moment there seemed to be a huge ear of corn on the motel bed, her hair the tassel. Keegan was almost relieved not to have to look at the body, she had been so lovely. He realized that Cy was tapping one hand with a notepad he held in the other.

"I thought you'd want to see this, Captain."

Keegan took the notepad. This must be the reason Cy had wanted him here. Across the top of the blank sheet was the name of the motel. Keegan turned it in the light and the indentations became visible. Numbers.

"Looks like an address."

"It is."

"Whose?"

"Father Dowling's. That's the number of the Saint Hilary rectory." Cy was right. Keegan shaded over the numbers with a pencil and there was Roger Dowling's address.

"No telling when it was written."

Horvath nodded. "Her name was Clare O'Leary. She lived within twenty miles of here. We've notified the police in Waukegan. They knew right off who she was."

"You mean she's been in trouble?"

"I gather she was a prominent person."

"She check in here alone?"

"That's right."

"Anybody notice anything?"

"You know motels. People don't know if someone is in the next room or not. Here today, gone tomorrow. The help aren't much better. Clean-up staff is around during the day, between changes of guests. They know someone has been here but they don't know who. It was the maid opening the door to clean the room who discovered the body. One o'clock is checkout time. She assumed the room had been vacated and was well inside before she noticed the body. She apologized and when she got no response thought something was wrong. When she realized the woman was dead she went screeching down the hall. Ganser nearly made a corpse out of her."

"No note?"

"The only thing is that tablet. There's the suitcase and an overnight bag. Oh, the television was on. That's why the maid didn't notice the body right away. She was looking toward the TV when she came in."

"When did the woman register?"

"Just before noon yesterday."

"Did she have any meals here in the motel? Did she do anything here?"

"We're still at that, of course. The bar, the coffee shop, the restaurant. There's a physical fitness center too. We'll check to see if she went there."

"Before committing suicide?"

"There's no note."

Cy was right. Those who choose to make their own exit from the world are likely to want to leave a message behind. It is the rare suicide who does not seek to have the last word.

"Maybe they'll find one at her home."

"Maybe."

Meanwhile they had the fact that someone who had occupied this room, perhaps the dead woman, had jotted down the number of St. Hilary's rectory on the pad beside the phone. But that could have been done days ago.

There was a sure way of finding out and, as Horvath must have guessed, Keegan was glad to pursue it. "I'll go talk to Father Dowling, Cy. Maybe he can throw some light on this."

3

ONCE, years ago, when he was in the Navy, Twinkie Zeugner had come back to the barracks drunk and started to break up the place with a bunch of other guys and got ten days in the brig from some son of a bitch of a commander who thought the new recruits were not as tough as they used to be. Those ten days had made Twinkie a poet of the deterrent theory of punishment. "Try living behind wire for a week," he would say. "Just try it. Heyzoo Christmas, man, it's like to drive you crazy." And he meant it. And that was why he found it so awful to be living in his cruddy room in the Stagecoach Inn on Jackson, outside Fox River. The room was like the others he had occupied in the Stagecoach chain—a box of space, no fresh air, phony décor, filled with loud-mouths in doubleknit clothes, and middle-aged women who thought they could giggle their way back to girlhood. What was his life but imprisonment? His routine was as rigid as the brig. Work his ass off in the Billet-Doux until three, asleep by four if he was lucky, and by seven the sound of showers running and voices in the hallway made restful sleep impossible. Ganser didn't like him having breakfast in the room. "Zeugner, you're a star. It's good to have the guests see you in the coffee shop. They recognize you from the display in the lobby. It makes for better business."

The middle-aged broads made a fuss over Twinkie, usually in pairs, sometimes in trios and quartets, just a few of the girls being naughty. Heyzoo Christmas, the gigglers. He couldn't stand the gigglers, but of course he had no choice. That brig time in the Navy had been a forecast of what lay ahead of him when he walked out the gate at Great Lakes, a civilian once again, free. Well, he was free of lots of things, but what was he free for?

When he got back to Iowa they said go to school, use the GI Bill and go to school. Study music, that's what his mother wanted. His father, after a short period of enjoying having Twinkie around again, obviously wanted him out from underfoot and if that meant going to school, okay, let him go to school. The big problem with this was that Twinkie knew all the music he needed. He just had the ear. The first time he sat down at a piano he had been able to pick out tunes. After a couple of months he had a repertoire. You name it, Twinkie could play it. He didn't know why he could do this, he just could. He didn't know a damned thing about notes and keys and the rest of it. After Twinkie's mother found out he could play the piano, she wanted him to take lessons, but a half an hour with Mrs. Powers was all Twinkie could stand. She confused the hell out of him. Before he left, he played a bit and Mrs. Powers just sat there with her mouth open.

So he wasn't likely to want to use the GI Bill to study music. One Saturday night, in a bar near Dubuque, Twinkie began to play the piano and made a huge hit. The owner of the bar offered him a job, Twinkie took it, joined the union. The rest, as he told the gigglers, was history.

He played in bars in the tri-city area for years, until he was twenty-four and Maxwell came through, stopped where Twinkie was playing, and called him over to his table between sets.

That was a scene as big in his life as getting ten days in the brig, only this had been good news. Twinkie skipped the first meeting with Maxwell, when he told the story of his life. For complicated reasons. Maybe there is some point like that in everyone's life, when you decide something and nothing is ever the same again afterward. Looking back, knowing what he now knew, Twinkie could still not wish he had stayed there in the tri-cities, maybe gone on home eventually. His life sure as hell would have been different. Heyzoo Christmas. That was more than twenty years ago and they had both been younger, Maxwell and himself. It wasn't Maxwell's clothes or the beard or the doll he was traveling with, no one thing, but Twinkie caught the scent of the big time. So he had a drink with Maxwell and his chick, they talked a bit about Twinkie's playing. Twinkie knew he was good. He had stopped being impressed by himself. He could play the piano in the way he was right-handed and had wavy hair and stood six feet four. It was just part of what he was. He asked the chick what she'd like to hear and played extra well that next set. Back at the table, Maxwell put an oval-shaped cigarette in his mouth and waited for the chick to light it.

"This is no place for you, Zeugner." Maxwell's words emerged like smoke signals. "You should be working in Chicago."

"I'm happy here. You gotta understand, I'm not a real musician."

Maxwell burst out laughing and the chick chirped in.

"I mean it. You put a sheet of music in front of me, I can't read it. I don't know from nothing. I hear a song, I can play it, that's all there is. I belong to the union, sure, but I'm no musician."

"Play 'Stardust.'"

He played "Stardust." He played all the Hoagie he knew and went on to Johnny Mercer. The chick wanted Eddie Howard, he gave her Eddie Howard. To each his own. Maxwell was staying overnight and he was determined he was going to hire Twinkie and take him back to Chicago.

"Look, I'll throw in Gladys. You want Gladys?"

The chick smiled. Twinkie thought they were kidding. He didn't take Gladys but he did take the job. Not that he "debouched," as Maxwell put it. He played out the week for the bar so they could get a replacement. By the time he boarded the bus for Chicago, he was worried Maxwell would have forgotten their deal. It had been only a handshake agreement and he had no guarantee Maxwell hadn't been drunk and would deny the whole thing. If he didn't remember Twinkie, Gladys sure as hell wasn't going to. That much he understood about those two.

Except that Gladys had been replaced by Magda by the time Twinkie got to Maxwell's lounge in the Loop. It was called the Stagecoach, as if Maxwell could already imagine the chain of motels he would build across northern Illinois and southern Wisconsin.

Stagecoach Inc. was a small empire, but it was an empire, and Maxwell stayed at the top, though how the hell he ever squared it with the mob Twinkie did not understand until his first long engagement at the inn near O'Hare.

By that time, Twinkie was on the stuff himself, bad. He still said he worked for Maxwell but the truth was he was his slave. Twinkie moved along the Stagecoach circuit, settling in for several months at each stop. Room, board, playing in the lounge. The coke was a fringe benefit. They said it was non-addictive, maybe that was why he had been willing to try it the first time. Well, they said cigarettes weren't addictive either, but Twinkie had never been able to quit for twenty-four hours in his life. Even so, if it came to cigarettes or coke, he would give up smoking first. He was hooked and the Stagecoach circuit assured him a steady and safe supply. People have sold their souls for less.

What he had never gotten used to was the gigglers. Where the hell do all these unattached middle-aged women come from and why the hell were they wall to wall in any lounge he played in? Figure it out, he told himself. These are the used cars of the marriage market, the wives discarded by all those middle-aged guys who want something new and something young. Where is a middle-aged woman going to find another husband when she couldn't hang onto the first one she had? Some of them did marry again or they got religion, but most of them seemed to hang around bars giggling and waiting for something to turn up. Twinkie received proposals of marriage on the average of once a week. He had never married. Gladys he hadn't gotten to know, really, but

Magda was a bitch and she was succeeded by a dozen other bitches and Twinkie wondered why Maxwell put up with them. Maxwell's girls had a way of reminding Twinkie of the girls in the personal-hygiene films he had been shown in boot camp and that was why he never accepted Maxwell's offer of a girl he'd tired of. And there was his Catholic training. Twinkie knew it was a sin to sleep with a girl. He didn't go to Mass anymore — how could he, given his schedule? He had stopped going to church back in the tri-cities but only because he was sleeping when Mass was being said. As far as he knew, he still believed it all, but he moved too much to have a parish, and now that he was on coke there was that as well. He would have to confess and say he was sorry and Twinkie knew there was no point, he couldn't give it up.

Clare had been a Catholic. There was that and the fact she didn't giggle, so they had gotten along fine. He sat with her between sets, sipped his Jack Daniels and listened. He was a great listener, not that he really followed what people were saying. People have to talk, they don't really need to be listened to. For some damned reason, they seemed to like his own story, and Clare was no exception.

"Do you ever get out of here, out of the motel?"

"Is there an outside?"

"You must get a day off."

"From what? I don't work. I play. I'm a musician."

"You do look as if you enjoy it."

"Don't you?"

She brought the burning tip of her cigarette toward his hand in mock menace. "Do you know 'Heartache'?"

"As well as I know heartburn."

He gave her the Les Paul/Mary Ford arrangement and she loved it. That was odd too. She wasn't old enough for that song.

The cop, Horvath, was almost as big as Twinkie and Twinkie could see the disapproval in the detective's eye. Clare had wondered if he left the motel much. The look in Horvath's eye was one reason he didn't. The thing is, he agreed with Horvath. It was a hell of a life he led and the cop didn't know the half of it.

"Clare?" Twinkie answered when Horvath asked if he knew her. "I don't think so."

"She was found dead in one of the units of the motel."

"Heyzoo Christmas! Dead?" It seemed the right reaction. If Horvath knew he already knew he would want to know how. Twinkie had gotten out of bed to open the door.

"She was in the lounge last night, where you play." Twinkie nodded, waiting for Horvath to go on. "Did you notice her?"

"You're kidding, right? You ever been in the Billet-Doux? That's the lounge. My own mother could be in there and I wouldn't know it. What happened to her?"

"Your mother?"

Twinkie laid a soft punch on Horvath's arm. "I'm going to order breakfast, want anything?" He would tell room service the order was Horvath's.

"No, thanks. How long you going to be playing here?"

Twinkie shrugged. "It's sort of open-ended at the moment. As long as they want me."

"Who decides?"

"The head honcho, Maxwell."

"He here in the motel?"

"The *head* honcho. The guy who owns the chain."

"I may want to talk with you again."

"Any time."

"What kind of a name is Twinkie?"

"They hung it on me when I was a kid. It was that or Junior. I'm stuck with it."

"Better order your breakfast."

"Right."

And Twinkie Zeugner closed the door on Lieutenant Horvath, picked up the phone, and dialed room service. Clare dead. Alone, he didn't have to pretend surprise. What was it he felt at the thought of her gone? Love? Heyzoo Christmas.

4

IN THE bar off the lobby of the Stagecoach Inn representatives of the local media were discussing the Harley killing — a natural association, since another body found in a motel had brought them here today. Mervel was nursing a Scotch and water in a highball glass, no ice, seething at the pontificating Wiggins. Wiggins, anchorman on the late night news on Channel 4, had arrived by helicopter. He wore a belted trench coat and a skeptical look. He was drinking sherry and Mervel found him a pain in the ass.

"How many deaths does this make? Fox River is becoming a charnel house."

"We're behind for the year," Mervel said. "In murders."

Wiggins's right brow lifted. "This was suicide."

He sipped his sherry. The man was an actor, not a reporter. But his face was pasted on billboards all over Fox River, grim smile, steely eyes, the intrepid newshound. Wiggins never said a word on camera that had not been written for him. While he sipped sherry, his photographer was taking footage around the motel and a girl in the lobby was writing Wiggins's words for the shot they would take of Wiggins at the scene of the newsbreak. Mervel had heard a guess on what they paid Wiggins and he prayed it was an exaggeration.

He said, "They always try suicide first."

"What do you mean?"

Wiggins must practice arching that right eyebrow.

"Of course the management will hold out for heart failure. Something natural." Mervel was trying to speak with weary worldliness, but his voice sounded phony even to himself.

"Is that right?" Wiggins moved his head slightly. He seemed to be regarding himself in the mirror behind the bar. A girl appeared in the doorway, silhouetted by the light from the lobby.

"Ready when you are, Bruce."

"Coming, dear."

Wiggins slid off the stool as if dismounting a just broken horse and headed for the lobby. Three quarters of his glass of sherry remained undrunk. Mervel exchanged a look with Ninian.

"Someday all the newspapers will be dead and the world will be in the hands of Wiggins."

Ninian reached for Wiggins's abandoned glass, brought it to his nose, then tasted it.

"Cough syrup."

Mervel sipped his Scotch as if he must rid his own mouth of the taste. He had half a mind to catch the late evening news to find out what Channel 4 would make of the motel suicide. He had phoned in his own account forty-five minutes before after talking with Phelps's assistant.

"Let's flip to see who goes to find out if they have an identification," Mervel suggested.

"Who's they? I saw Keegan leave twenty minutes ago and there goes Horvath now."

Mervel got off his stool somewhat less gracefully than Wiggins had and emerged blinking into the lobby. He caught Horvath before he went outside to where the patrol car was waiting for him.

"Who was she, Horvath?"

"Don't know. You got the name?"

"How did she spell it?" Never admit ignorance was a rule Mervel followed faithfully.

"The first name. C-l-a-r-e. The last one she spells like Mrs. O'Leary's cow."

"How did you track that down?"

"We looked in her purse."

Mervel was taking notes. The story he had phoned in was all shot to hell. Unidentified beauty found dead of overdose of sleeping pills in local motel. He liked the note of mystery in his stories. Vagueness about facts contributed to the mystery of his style.

"Where does she live, Horvath?"

"She lived in Waukegan."

Mervel squinted at Horvath. "That close? Then why's she staying here?"

Horvath shrugged.

"Sounds like she came here to kill herself."

Horvath shrugged again. No matter. Mervel did not need police authorization to pursue the story line he had suggested. Horvath turned and pushed through the door and went outside. Mervel went back across the lobby toward the phones. Halfway down a corridor bright lights illumined Bruce Wiggins as he spoke earnestly into the camera. Mervel entered the phone booth as if it were a haven against the likes of Wiggins.

Mervel put down the phone. What the hell did he know about the woman anyway? Nothing. He stepped out of the booth. The curly-haired giant who played piano in the Billet-Doux Lounge had come into the lobby and was chatting with several women who had risen from their chairs at his appearance. Mervel went to the desk.

"Is Ganser in?"

"I can take a message," the girl said.

"I'll tell him myself."

He rounded the counter and strode purposefully to Ganser's door. He knocked with one hand and turned the knob with the other. Ganser sat behind his desk, a phone pressed to his ear. At the sight of Mervel, he cupped his cigarette, took the phone from his ear, and pressed the receiver against his chest.

"Get the hell out of here! This is a private office."

Mervel smiled and sat down. He had all the leverage he needed from the smell of what Ganser was smoking.

5

HER HAIR had gone gray in a way other women paid lots to dupli-
cate in the beauty parlor, but all Andrea Kohler had to do was
wash it and have it trimmed from time to time. No more trouble
than a man's. Well, some men's. Larry spent more time and money
on his hair than any two women she knew. Sometimes she wondered what he would do if he were on television rather than radio.
His fortune was his voice, rich, the promise of laughter just beneath the surface, a forceful reassuring voice. Like so many others,
she had been conquered by that voice long before she laid eyes on
him. When she did, she learned how idealized the photos of him
were, the ones that seemed everywhere, on the side of panel trucks,
on billboards, in the newspaper. Larry O'Leary, with music you
love to hear. That such a voice should emerge from his slight
body with its pot, rounded and stooped shoulders, and the inexo-
rably thinning hair, teased and sprayed and coaxed into some
semblance of its former self, was one of life's mysteries.

The program of his she favored was, she came to learn, an
instance of a minor national trend, music from the forties and
fifties, the big bands, singers who could sing, Margaret Whiting,
Helen O'Connell, the Ames Brothers. She had been driving back
from Milwaukee the first time she happened on the station and
she had no protection against the memories evoked without warning by the voice of Dick Haymes singing "It Might As Well Be
Spring." She actually cried, her eyes blurring so that she had to

pull into a rest area. How long had she sat there on that bright December day, listening to music that seemed to cancel decades, take away the failures, bring back those wonderful years when she had been a woman?

That was how she put it. When I was a woman. I used to be a lady. One whole hell of a lot had happened to her since those days, things that forced upon her the enormous unconscious plot against women. Her view of herself had been assimilated from the culture. She had accepted a subservient position because, after all, she was a woman. Jack, of course, was the man, and that meant her life was tied to his and whither he goest she went too. Dutifully. And, admit it, happily. That was the worst thing about the indoctrination; she had really believed it and was content to be a woman, Jack's wife, Number Two for life, second class. She had borne her three children, they were nothing if not the average family, two girls for her, a boy for Jack. They had lived in West Allis, then moved to New Berlin, both decisions of Jack's.

Those were the years of those songs, more or less. Their vogue had been prolonged for them because Jack was ten years older than she, his record collection was immense, and he had always been the first in line when something new in stereo equipment came out. She did her housework surrounded by sound. Jack had speakers upstairs, downstairs, in every room. There was an ideology in those lyrics, a notion of what a woman is, one that some jazz records contradicted only in part. Anita O'Day was not the voice of the liberated woman, even if her name was pig Latin for money.

When had she stopped being a woman? In retrospect she pinned it to a dinner party at which for the first time she realized Jack's condescension toward her. They had been talking of the Kennedy years and Andrea thought she remembered those times as well as anyone at the table, but when she spoke Jack publicly shushed her up. And nobody paid any attention to what he had done. After all, she was his wife. Him Tarzan, she Jane. It took her out of herself and gave her a quick disturbing look at her life.

She began to notice other things, the way the kids treated her, for example. She had her definite range of authority; no one contested that the kitchen was hers, preparing the meals, keeping the house clean, even allotting the cars. But serious matters were discussed with Jack. This was as true of the girls as it was of Jack, Junior. Jack, Junior! It had been Andrea who insisted on naming their son after Jack. But there was no little Andrea, just Nancy and Grace. Not that she had wanted a daughter named after her; it wasn't that. But why was it all right for Jack and not for her?

Andrea had brooded in her perfect kitchen in her immaculate house in the lovely suburb; she sipped coffee and reviewed her life. She was then about to turn thirty-four. There did not seem to be one single aspect of her personality that was herself alone. She was exhausted by external relations: wife of Jack, mother of Jack, Junior and Nancy and Grace. And other relations — daughter, sister, aunt, and niece. But who was she herself?

It was the kind of question they had been urged to put to themselves during retreat at school. What does God want me to do? What special calling is mine? For one or two girls that question had led to the convent, but the rest of them knew the answer would be married life. She would meet the man who would become her husband and the father of her children and live happily ever after in this life and be happy with God in the next. When in her mid-thirties she looked her life in the eye and permitted herself to entertain the possibility that she had been conned since childhood, her self-definition had begun. Influences? She honestly was not aware of any. She didn't make a big thing of it but she was certain she had thought her way out of happy servitude unaided by anyone else. She had drawn strength from Betty.

After graduation, Betty had become a postulant and eventually Sister Mary Catherine. Andrea had been fairly close to Betty, they had doubled a few times, and Betty's decision to become a nun had made Andrea uneasy, as if she too might be drawn into that life of self-abnegation and be deprived of the husband and family she wanted. Betty had been Sister Mary Catherine for ten years when she had had enough. Andrea got the news from her in a phone call that really shocked her. It had never dawned on her that nuns could stop being nuns.

"You're kidding," Betty said, when they met in the bar of the Bronson Hotel. "Haven't you been reading the papers?"

Andrea had expected a timid woman, furtive, overwhelmed by a world she had left years before. But Betty looked as if she were on top of the world.

Her hair was parted in the middle, worn not too long, and there was a thread or two of gray in it that looked good. The hair-do was clearly designed to do something about the narrowness of her face. The glasses helped too: large lenses gave her eyes a sort of surprised amusement that went with the sardonic smile. And she smoked a cigarette with her margarita. Andrea had the un-settling sense that it was she who had been out of things for years and Betty who had been in the thick of what was happening. She had taken part in protests, she had marched, there had even been an arrest, but no detention.

"As soon as they found out I was a nun, they let me go. I felt cheated."

But it was the treatment of women in the Church that had finally gotten to Betty. Andrea wasn't too sure she agreed with her. Women priests? That was silly. Her own religious faith be-gan to go for other reasons, and within a year it was gone entirely. Apparently Betty's went too. She married a divorced man and moved to Honolulu where, in the sun and surf and affluence of her life, she soon forgot the many causes that had brought her over the convent wall. By that time Andrea, to Jack's stunned surprise, to the mixed amusement and pride of the kids, had moved into an apartment near the Marquette campus and begun the study of law.

Jack had put the Jesuits onto her as a confused woman who had abandoned her family, but the young theologian she was visited by did nothing to dissuade her from her intention to be a lawyer. Why law? Because law is the principal instrument of change in society and Andrea meant to do what she could to bring other women to the point she herself had reached. That was before she realized that most women couldn't care less about their status in society. They liked the suburban life: long lunches after a strenuous morning in the shopping mall, bridge, golf, and dinner parties to advance a husband's career. What was so wrong with that?

"Not a damned thing if that is what you want," became Andrea's answer. She gave up all thought of becoming the apostle to the enslaved women of America. Let them eat cake. She had to live her own life, and after she passed the bar that is what she did. Lesson One was the realization that the big firms did not want to take on a woman her age. It wasn't said out loud and there was a certain justification for it: they wanted to train people who had a long career ahead of them, and Andrea was now perilously close to forty. The lack of interest of the large firms had been a blessing in disguise. She opened her own office. The thought returned that she might specialize in the legal problems of women or minorities. It frightened her, looking back, that she might actually have done that. She would have been frustrated and broke. She decided to make a bundle instead. Independence was rooted in money. Not that she hadn't stuck Jack good in the divorce settlement. Why shouldn't she? She had been a big help to him and he knew it.

It was too bad about Jack. More than anger, more than resentment, Jack felt embarrassment that she had left him. He was ashamed. So he opted for early retirement, moved out of Milwaukee, and was now involved in a second career in Tampa. Jack, Junior had joined him there and apparently the two of them were doing very well. Andrea did not like to think of her son. The mere memory of him made her feel hated. The girls were married and happy, male chauvinists, both of them. Ah, well. Maybe that was her gift to them. If she had stayed happy as a wife and mother her daughters might have become rebels. As it was, they were flaming conservatives, in politics, in religion. Larry would love them. They were his kind of Catholic.

The move to Waukegan had been made in her second year of practice. She took the Illinois bar and moved south and it was the real start of her career. No one knew her. She was on her own. And she flourished. She discovered in herself a capacity to be really tough. And she attracted clients. Larry O'Leary had helped there, though he seemed almost jealous of other clients, as if she should be his private lawyer. He couldn't have afforded that, though she didn't tell him. She was in her way an expert on the male ego. It was a good part of the reason for her success. But she was grateful to Larry, and Nan her secretary had standing instructions to put his calls right through. That is why she had been interrupted to take his call about Clare.

"Oh no, Larry!"

"I just got the call from Fox River. She was found dead in a motel there."

"What happened?"

"'Self-inflicted' was the way they put it."

"My God. Clare. I can't believe it."

"What should I do?"

It was absurd that his voice did not betray any emotion but was the same modulated instrument with which he carried on his patter between records or interviewed guests on his talk show. "I'll go with you, of course."

"I've cleared everything here. There is lots of stuff on tape. I told them I'd come as soon as possible."

"Look, I'll drive. Do you want me to pick you up at the studio?"

"I'm calling from home. Father Hogan is here with me."

"Good. It won't be more than fifteen minutes."

Of course Larry would have called a priest before he called his lawyer. She could predict the conversation they would have on the drive to Fox River. Larry was going to worry about the state of his wife's immortal soul. Well, he would have to consult with Hogan about that. But after she hung up, she sat back for a moment and thought of Clare. Clare hadn't liked her and Andrea had not been wild about Clare. Wives had difficulty when their husbands treated other women as equals; Andrea understood that, she used to be a woman herself. And she was sorry Clare was dead. After a moment's silence it was over. Andrea Kohler did not intend to pretend a grief she did not feel. She was sure Larry would handle that side of things fully. Larry the widower. This made him free.

But it was the last will she had drawn up for him that she thought of as she drove to the O'Leary home.

6

MARIE MURKIN'S reaction to the death of Clare O'Leary was in inverse proportion to the dislike she had felt for the woman when she came to the St. Hilary rectory. She had made her views known in little bursts of comment when she served dinner that night and later when Phil Keegan was there. She let it be known that, as for herself, she thought women ought to dress their age, not try to look like schoolgirls all their lives. Take hair, for instance. Did any woman over thirty have the right to wear her hair long? Phil Keegan couldn't think of any statutes against it. Marie ignored him. She couldn't remember when she had last seen a camel's-hair coat. And loafers? Mrs. Murkin's laugh was far from merry. When was it loafers had been in style?

Roger Dowling and Phil Keegan exchanged a glance. There was only one response to Mrs. Murkin's monologue. They turned on the Cubs.

The following day Phil told the priest that the body of a woman named Clare O'Leary had been found in the Stagecoach Inn.

"Dear God," Father Dowling said. Marie, who had come in from the kitchen, blessed herself when she connected the name with yesterday's visitor and, with a stricken look, disappeared.

"How did it happen, Phil?" Roger Dowling eased himself into his chair behind the desk and reached for his pipe. Phil took the chair in which Mrs. O'Leary had sat not much more than twenty-four hours before. Do we ever stop being surprised by mortality?

"Sleeping pills."

Roger Dowling stopped the lighted match halfway to the bowl of his pipe. "Sleeping pills! Surely she didn't take her own life?"

Phil carefully unwrapped the cigar he had taken from his pocket and lit it. "Your address had been written on the pad beside the bed. Was it Clare O'Leary who wrote it?"

"She came to see me yesterday."

"Can you tell me why?"

"I can tell you that suicide was the last thing from her mind."

"What was on her mind?"

Roger Dowling struck another match and this time lit his pipe. While he puffed it into life, he considered how he might answer. Confidences survive those who entrust us with them and Clare O'Leary had spoken to him in confidence. She had left her husband, run away from home, hidden in a motel. He could tell Phil that. But he would hesitate to repeat what she had said about her husband. He realized that he did not believe her story about those threats.

"She wanted to talk to a priest."

"She drove here from Waukegan and registered in a motel so she could have a talk with you?"

"It could have been any priest."

"And you can't tell me what it was about?"

"Phil, she had left her husband. At least she thought she had. I was going to see her again today. She imagined she was regaining her freedom." His voice dropped in comment on her hopes.

"Roger, the woman apparently committed suicide. That is technically a crime, but it's hard to prosecute people for doing it."

"Would you like a beer?"

"Of course I'd like a beer. But I think I'll have a cup of coffee instead."

"You're on duty."

"That has nothing to do with it."

When the coffee was poured, Roger Dowling said, "Tell me all about it, Phil."

Roger Dowling knew where the Stagecoach Inn was. Clare O'Leary could have found a closer priest. Had he been of any help to her? Not if she committed suicide, certainly, but he found it impossible to believe she had. His image of the motel was of a sooty place on the edge of the roar of Jackson Avenue. Hardly a restful place, certainly not where one would choose to exit from the world. Had she gone back there from the rectory with the intention of taking her life? If she could be believed, she feared for her life, in flight from a husband she said intended to have her killed. Phil spoke on dispassionately of the body on the bed, of Phelps's characteristic caution in seconding the verdict of suicide.

"Did he have any reason to hesitate, Phil?"

"Phelps? Of course. The laws of nature may have been abrogated and he would be left out on a limb. Just because sleeping pills taken by the dozen have caused deaths in the past is no reason to feel confident they will go on doing so. Not that he has another theory. He is wary of any explanation. Roger, a rank amateur would have known it was suicide within five minutes."

"What have you learned about her?"

"Cy and Agnes Lamb are working on that. She was from Waukegan, as you must know, and a prominent citizen. Her husband has been informed.

"I'd like to meet him."

"Why?"

"Just to tell him that I spoke to his wife. Was I the last one she spoke to, I wonder."

"Won't you tell him his wife had run away from home?"

"I suppose he'll know that already, Phil."

Phil Keegan had the look of a man who would like a verbatim account of Roger Dowling's conversation with Clare O'Leary. What Dowling had not told him, Phil would soon learn — *if* Clare's story was true. Phil seemed put off by his old friend's reticence, but when the call came from Cy Horvath saying the woman's husband had arrived, he asked Roger Dowling to come along.

"You don't mind if I introduce you as chaplain of the Police Department, do you, Roger?"

"I'd be flattered."

"O'Leary," Keegan mused. "He's either a Catholic or he should be."

Larry O'Leary and his counsel were brought from the morgue to Phil Keegan's office and it was there that Roger Dowling got his first look at two people of whom Clare O'Leary had said such extraordinary things.

Larry O'Leary was not at all as he had imagined him from his wife's story but then, the celebrity of Waukegan radio was not in a situation in which he could be expected to be at his best. He had just come from viewing the body of his dead wife and was doubtless in a numbed condition. The handsome, self-assured woman with him did most of O'Leary's talking, explaining that she and her client had conferred on the drive to Fox River. Her splendid silver hair was even more dramatic because of the black velvet jacket she wore. She seemed at once to use her beauty and to be contemptuous of it. Here was a woman who wished to be admired for her mind. She did not seem at all the person Clare O'Leary had described as having an affair with her husband, if only because Larry O'Leary was such an unprepossessing man. What could have been his attraction for her? Surely not that, within a finite range of Waukegan, his voice was famous. Andrea Kohler did not strike Father Dowling as a woman who would rest easy in the shadow of another's accomplishments. The sight of the priest's Roman collar gave her only momentary pause.

"Oh, good. Larry will appreciate your being here."

That seemed true enough. O'Leary enclosed Roger Dowling's hand in both of his and looked at the priest with tear-filled eyes.

"Pray for me, Father."

Roger Dowling nodded and retrieved his hand. It was

difficult to know how to take the remark. There was a bandying about of such phrases — risqué comics ending their acts with a "God Bless." But that was unfair. He must not see Larry O'Leary only through his dead wife's eyes. There was no reason to doubt his sincerity. But he could not forget how Clare had described her husband's religiosity.

Larry O'Leary had last seen his wife at breakfast the day before. There had been nothing in her manner or in what she said to suggest she planned to do what she had done. No quarrels? He shook his head.

"Their marriage was the envy of those who knew them," Andrea Kohler said. "I speak as a friend rather than as counsel when I say that."

Roger Dowling said, "Did you, as a friend of Mrs. O'Leary, have any inkling this might happen?"

"Clare O'Leary was one of the most fortunate women I knew. I can more easily imagine myself committing suicide than I can Clare."

"You don't think it was suicide?"

Her eyes flew to Keegan and Horvath, but she directed her question to Roger Dowling. "Is there any reason to doubt it was suicide?"

"Is there, Phil?" Roger Dowling tried to keep his voice disingenuous.

"It was an accident," Larry O'Leary announced. For the first time Father Dowling could believe he was what his wife had said, a radio personality. There was such conviction in the voice that it invited belief. "Clare and I are Catholics, Father. She did not commit suicide."

Andrea Kohler nodded as if at a self-evident truth. Roger Dowling wished it were. The other side of O'Leary's confidence was the dread accompanying the thought that a loved one had taken her own life, committed the sin of despair.

"I saw her yesterday, Mr. O'Leary. She came to my rectory. I must say I share your disbelief that she committed suicide."

"She came to see you?" Andrea Kohler said. "Had you known her?"

"She wanted to talk to a priest and chose me. She did say she had heard of me. I can't imagine where."

"What did she want to talk about?" O'Leary's voice contained many emotions at once. Roger Dowling looked around the office and smiled apologetically.

"We could talk of that in private if you wish."

"Of course I do. You may have been the last one she spoke to, Father. I want to know everything she said."

"Mr. O'Leary, the official verdict is self-inflicted death." Phil Keegan spoke softly.

"I don't give a damn about that," O'Leary said, an improbably Churchillian voice rumbling from his narrow chest. "Self-inflicted death! How mealy-mouthed. At least you're ashamed to come right out and say it. 'Suicide' is the word, Captain, and it does not apply to my wife."

"The medical examiner makes those judgments, Mr. O'Leary, not us."

"Well, he's wrong. Father, where can we talk?"

Finding a room in which to talk was less of a problem than establishing that Larry O'Leary did not need counsel with him while he talked with a priest.

"Do you mind, Larry?" Andrea Kohler said when Roger Dowling suggested this would be a confidential matter.

"It's simply that Mrs. O'Leary told me things in confidence. If Mr. O'Leary wants to tell you later, that will be his decision. But you understand my position."

"Are you saying Clare went to confession to you?"

"If she had, I could not speak of that with anyone."

"Of course not," Larry O'Leary said. "Andrea, you'd better let me talk with Father alone. We can talk later."

"You may not want to pass on everything your wife said to me, Mr. O'Leary," Roger Dowling said when he had closed the door of Phil Keegan's office.

O'Leary's manner altered when they were alone. He sighed, shook a cigarette loose, and extended the package to Father Dowling.

"No, thanks."

"Do you mind if I smoke?"

"Certainly not."

Larry lit up and exhaled a massive cloud of smoke. "I didn't want to tell the police more than I had to, Father. If you talked with Clare, you'll know what I mean."

"Perhaps you'd better tell me."

O'Leary looked both pained and thoughtful. "Father, it's hard to sit here talking about her. Dead." He shook his head and tears ran from his eyes. "God bless her soul, Father. She was truly a good woman and a good wife. I feel responsible for this."

"In what way?"

"What I told the police, what Andrea said about Clare, well, that wasn't the real picture. Clare was a very troubled woman. Father, she accused me of having an affair with Andrea — my lawyer! — and she had convinced herself that I wanted to kill her."

"Kill Andrea?"

"No, no. Clare, my wife. She thought I meant to kill her. I thought she might have said these things to you."

"Had she said them to anyone else?"

"Yes. To another priest. Do you know Father Hogan?"

"Yes, I know him, perhaps not well."

"I do. He is a very dear friend of mine — I think I can say that. Clare went to him with the story I just told you. Can you imagine?"

Roger Dowling was wondering how O'Leary had come to know what his wife had said to a priest.

"She told me she had," O'Leary said, as if reading his thoughts. "She seemed surprised he didn't believe her."

"Why on earth would she think a thing like that?"

"If it isn't true? Believe me, Father, it's not true. Obviously Clare needed professional help and I should have made sure she got it. I didn't and I'll never forgive myself."

"She did tell me those things, Mr. O'Leary. I must say she didn't seem unbalanced in any way."

"I know! That is what was so eerie about it. Listening to her I could half believe I was running around with Andrea and looking for hired killers to get rid of Clare. She must have had some kind of death wish. Basically, I think, it's because we never had children. She could never accept that. It made her feel inadequate. I told her it was just as likely a deficiency of mine, but that didn't help. The Church is right, Father. Women are born to be mothers. If they can't have children of their own there has to be some substitute. Clare wouldn't hear of adoption, however — it would have been a public admission of defeat. I think she would have preferred people to think we had decided against children, that we were practicing birth control, rather than have them know we were incapable. That is what she resented in Andrea. Andrea has children."

"Does your lawyer know of your wife's suspicions?"

"I'm afraid so, Father. Three of us knew Clare's real condition: Father Hogan, myself, and Andrea. But the responsibility was mine. It's a blessing really that Father Hogan knew."

"How do you mean?"

"Well, he won't refuse her a Church burial, will he? Knowing what he did about her?"

7

THE ADONIS & Aphrodite Physical Fitness Center was a bonus of the Stagecoach chain and Maxwell went to some trouble in selecting managers for each of the centers, making the choice personally. Wilma Goudge had been the manager of the A & A in the Stagecoach Inn on Jackson Avenue for a year and a half and she was as good an advertisement for its wares as could be asked.

She gave her age as twenty-four although she would never see thirty again. Twinkie told her she could have passed for nineteen, but Twinkie was full of beans.

"It should be Aphrodite & Adonis," he said to her the first time they talked.

"Why?"

"Ladies first."

"Isn't Adonis the woman?"

"If you can't tell the difference, I don't think I want a massage from you."

That was one thing Wilma took no kidding about. Under her management the physical fitness center was what it claimed to be and nothing more. Her massages were the real thing, not just a cheap thrill, and she wanted Twinkie to get that straight right away.

"I was just feeling you out."

"Can that, Twinkie. I mean it."

"Okay, okay. Want some?"

"What is it?"

"Coke."

"Not on your life. I'm clean and I'm staying that way."

"Good for you."

"You should take care of yourself. Why mess around with that stuff?"

"It's not addictive."

"You could land in the slammer."

"Don't even think that."

Twinkie worked out every day and his body was in great shape. They made a pair, Wilma told herself, from the point of view of physical fitness anyway. Wilma didn't have an ounce of fat on her, though she had weight where it counts. She had not made the mistake some girls do of building up her muscles. A woman with muscles is a freak and that's all there is to it. Wilma exercised in order to emphasize that her body was female. She expected Twinkie to make a pass at her after that beginning but apparently he was only a talker. The guy lived like a monk and that, Wilma believed, was unhealthy. She did not favor promiscuity, far from it, but neither did she think we should let our gender atrophy. She thought she had gotten the message through to Twinkie, but he wasn't receiving. He wasn't queer, she was sure of that. If it wasn't for the coke she would have thought he was religious. And, Oh my God! could he play the piano.

Wilma did not drink. She would not do that to her body any more than she would have smoked cigarettes, but she had acquired the habit of spending hours listening to Twinkie play and she did not mind the smoke and smell of liquor in the lounge. She drank diet soda and just dreamed through his sets. Why didn't they still write music of the kind Twinkie played every night in the Billet-Doux? Of course Twinkie punned on the name.

"Many girl talk, but Billie do."

"Just name the time and place, Twinkie," she said boldly.

"Now, now. I won't corrupt you."

Or anyone else, apparently. Wilma made a little project of it, keeping an eye on him to see if there was someone in his life. In the lounge, he was surrounded by unattached females. He seemed to love it but he never took one of them to his room or went to theirs, at least as far as Wilma could find out. It was puzzling. If he ever were going to change his habits, she figured it would be with the O'Leary woman.

When they found her dead in the motel, Wilma's first thought was that there would be a note professing love for Twinkie and despair that it would never be returned. The thought was prompted by Wilma's reading. She devoured five Gothic romances a week, lying on the exercise bench in the physical fitness center on slack days or swiveling in her chair in the little office at the end of the gym.

"Did she leave a note?"

Twinkie looked at her as if he didn't have the remotest idea what she was talking about. My God, didn't he know the O'Leary woman was dead? If he didn't, Wilma wasn't going to be the one to tell him. Let Ganser do it. Let the police.

"What do you mean, leave a note? You think maybe she committed suicide? Forget it. She was raised Catholic, same as me."

"You were raised Catholic?"

"That's right."

So that was it. That seemed to explain a lot of things about Twinkie Zeugner.

"I thought I heard that's what happened."

"Maybe you did. But that couldn't have been it."

"What do you think happened?"

He shrugged and his eyes looked odd, almost misty. "Maybe she had a heart attack or something. I don't know. She was in the lounge last night, listening to me play. She had a couple of drinks, made a lot of requests. She was in a very good mood."

"I know, I know. I was there myself."

"Okay. So that wasn't a woman getting ready to go to her room and take her own life, was it?"

"I guess you're right." Wilma said it but she wasn't sure she meant it.

"I suppose that's the way to handle it, though. If the authorities want to call it a suicide I guess we can all pretend we never knew her. It can't hurt her, not now. Just let the whole thing be forgotten."

"Who knew her besides you?"

He was lifting barbells, right hand, left hand, slowly, getting the maximum advantage out of it. "You're kidding, aren't you, Wilma?"

"Am I?"

"Don't you really know who she came to see?"

"The amount of time she spent in the Billet-Doux, I'd say you."

"Anyone comes into the lounge sees me. That doesn't mean I'm the reason they're there." A thoughtful smile moved slowly across Twinkie's face. "All right, I gotcha. And you're right. See no evil, speak no evil." He nodded as if they had just entered into a pact.

Wilma honestly hadn't the faintest idea what he was talking about, but his assumption that she was being careful suggested possibilities that seemed pretty far out. The way Twinkie was acting you'd think Mrs. O'Leary had been meeting Maxwell here. That was a thought best left unpursued. She really felt now the caution Twinkie had attributed to her. It was unhealthy to know too much about Maxwell's life, personal or business. Twinkie felt the same way, obviously, and he and Maxwell had known each other for years. She had heard Twinkie referred to as Maxwell's protégé. But she could not stop her thoughts so easily. Had Maxwell ever been here at the motel when Mrs. O'Leary was registered? Wilma could remember at least three different occasions when Mrs. O'Leary had stayed in the motel.

"Maybe it was an overdose, Twinkie."

"You think the medical examiner would miss a thing like that?"

"Did she use the stuff?"

Twinkie looked at her, just looked at her, and it would have been difficult to say what his expression meant. But Wilma felt fear such as she had not felt in a long time. She did not like that. The great advantage of working for Maxwell was the sense of security it gave her. The Stagecoach system was large enough to have treaties with those who really ran things and small enough not to be perceived as serious competition. That did not mean Maxwell was a crook necessarily or that the Stagecoach system was not what it seemed. Wilma would not have worked here if she thought it was just a front. She was dedicated to the concept of health through exercise. The body is sacred. If she did not smoke or drink, she sure wasn't going to get caught up in other exploitations of the human body. Selling sex and drugs were o-u-t, period.

Twinkie's habit was just one of things you expect from musicians. He had offered her coke out of misguided friendliness. As far as Wilma could tell, the rest of the staff was clean. Ganser was a secret drinker — if something everyone knew about could count as a secret — but that was a personal fault, not a policy. In both its bars, this motel, like others in Maxwell's chain, sold drinks but did not hustle them. The aim was not to get the customer drunk. Wilma had never seen a drunk in the Billet-Doux. Some tipsy women, sure, but nothing gross. Wilma felt that her physical fitness work fitted into the general image of the motel. She was happy here. But Twinkie's steady gaze after she made the dumb remark about Mrs. O'Leary threatened to destroy her sense of security. It was a reminder: these were not things one casually discussed.

"I'm sorry. I shouldn't have said that."

"I never heard it." He resumed lifting barbells and, after a discreet minute or two, Wilma beat it back to her office at the end of the gym. Twinkie might look like a big teddy bear but she wondered if he really was. His stupid nickname encouraged people to think he was harmless. Maybe he was. But when she asked him if Clare had been hooked on drugs, he had looked as if he could kill her. She did not ever want Twinkie to look at her like that again.

8

HE TRIED to explain it to Cy Horvath, he tried to explain it to Marie Murkin, but he just couldn't find the right words. He actually hesitated to tell Roger Dowling the sympathy he felt for Larry O'Leary. On the surface, it was surprising that Phil Keegan, a Fox River cop, should feel the kind of identity he did with a Waukegan disc jockey with thinning hair, a barrel of a voice, and a hair-do that normally would have gotten a snicker from Phil Keegan. Like many men whose hair was still thick, Phil imagined he would have gone bald gracefully and without complaint. Better that than to brush your hair against the grain to try to cover up the baldness. It suggested vanity, a feminine weakness, a lack of the qualities Phil Keegan insisted on in men. There was O'Leary's voice to make up for it, of course, but that wasn't the explanation. He had told Cy and Mrs. Murkin he thought O'Leary was handling his wife's death about as well as could be expected, but neither of them would have understood he was thinking of his own wife's death. That was what attracted Phil Keegan to O'Leary. They were fellow widowers.

"He talks too damned much," Cy said evenly.

"That's how he makes his living."

But Cy had never lost a wife. When Phil Keegan lost his, he had become more taciturn than before and his daughters, though more demonstrative, like their mother, had understood. If he had acted out of character then he would have caused them more, not less, grief. The same with O'Leary, if you follow me, as Mrs. Murkin didn't.

She sat at the kitchen table, chewing on her lower lip, staring beyond Phil Keegan at the lowering sky visible through the kitchen window. She had not really been listening to him. There were tears in her eyes. You would have thought she was in mourning herself, and in a way, a crazy way, she was.

"The way I treated that woman. And talked about her. God forgive me, Phil Keegan. She was within hours of her death and I all but turned her away from the door. There's that at least, she saw a priest before she died."

Keegan frowned and sipped his coffee. He did not like the emphasis put on the wife. He was beginning to doubt that Clare O'Leary was at all the sort of person Marie Murkin now chose to remember. Things were coming to light at the Stagecoach and Phil Keegan did not like them at all. For one thing, they disturbed the parallel between his own loss and O'Leary's. Keegan's wife had died a Christian death in her own bed, not in a motel of which they knew too many unsavory things already and were now learning more. Marie Murkin seemed to suggest that Clare O'Leary had been in the process of making a religious retreat at the Stagecoach Inn, stopping by the St. Hilary parish house for instruction and then darting back to her cell of a room. Well, let the housekeeper have such pious thoughts, even if she did use them to whip up her own sense of guilt at the way she had treated the O'Leary woman when she showed up at the door.

So there were reasons why he had not talked at any length with Roger Dowling about the similarity between what had happened to the radio personality of Waukegan and Phil Keegan. To himself at least he could mention the staunch religious faith that set O'Leary off from others. Not that he was sanctimonious. Phil Keegan could not have taken a minute of him if he were. Little pious remarks were all right coming from Marie Murkin, as they had been from the lips of his departed wife, but men did not divulge their religious sentiments like that. No, O'Leary had a matter-of-fact way of referring to his Catholic beliefs that Keegan found manly and right. It was the way he himself would have talked about his faith if he were the talkative type. O'Leary was different from Roger Dowling on that score, Phil Keegan did not know quite how, but that was to be expected. After all, Roger Dowling was a priest.

It was O'Leary's friendship with Father Hogan that first gave Phil the idea that he and O'Leary had a lot in common. He had looked up the priest when he went to Waukegan. Father Hogan ("Call me Dave!") was a far cry from Roger Dowling, of course. He was bright and breezy, an elbow squeezer when he shook your hand, and his blue eyes twinkled behind the fancy glasses. Egg bald, so it was hard to know how old he was. The corners of his mouth turned down when he smiled and he stepped back to grin knowingly at Phil Keegan.

"He sounds more like a friend than a parishioner."

Hogan nodded. "Oh, yes, Larry and I go way back. He called me first thing when he heard about Clare."

"What did he say? I mean, how did he put it?"

Father Hogan did not let the regular interval elapse before lighting another cigarette. There was a pained expression on his face and he swiveled in his modernistic chair and looked at the one meager bookshelf. "Captain, there are things you should know about Clare."

"That's why I'm here."

"Then you've already heard?" Hogan looked relieved. Keegan shook his head and the sad expression returned.

"I'm here to learn all I can about a suicide in my jurisdiction. Mainly because O'Leary refuses to believe it was suicide. Father, there doesn't seem to be much doubt of that."

"I'm not surprised. Captain, tell me just what you do know about Clare."

What they knew was that she had checked into the Stagecoach Motel in Fox River, looked up Roger Dowling's address in the phone book, and gone to see him. She had given Roger Dowling no reason to think she contemplated suicide. She returned to the motel, spent some time in the show lounge of the motel before retiring. She was found dead the following afternoon at one-thirty by the maid. Death had been due to an overdose of sleeping pills, and the judgment was that it was self-inflicted.

"It wasn't an accident that she went to Roger Dowling. I am almost certain I mentioned his name to her. He was a kind of hero of mine in the seminary, the admiration of someone on the bottom of the ladder for a man soon to be ordained. And he was brilliant, effortlessly brilliant, and his class was full of geniuses. Even then, everyone seemed to think Roger Dowling was destined to be a bishop. He was sent on to study canon law, and that seemed right. If it had been theology it would have looked as though he was destined for the seminary faculty. But canon law is the sort of thing a future bishop should be expert in. When he was appointed to the marriage court, it looked even more like a sure thing. His drinking destroyed all that, of course. It was because I heard he had overcome his problem that I mentioned him to Clare O'Leary. I never thought I would refer to Roger Dowling as a tragic figure."

"You told Mrs. O'Leary about him?" Why would Hogan tell the woman things that made Roger Dowling seem altogether different from the man Phil Keegan knew? And not at all the person Hogan claimed to remember. Tragic figure? The proper response to that was "Bullshit" but, though Keegan felt Hogan would not resent the expletive, he did not blurt it out. Hogan leaned toward him, sincere.

"It wasn't gossip, Captain. I might be fine for Larry but I knew I was not the priest Clare needed. It's been years since I've seen Roger, but I was certain he could get through to her."

"What was her problem?"

"I'll tell you because I know Larry will if he already hasn't. She was a strange woman. Sometimes I thought she was on something, drugs, but according to Larry she never went beyond Valium. And sleeping pills." Hogan grimaced. "Whatever the cause, she was a flake. I can tell you in the privacy of this room that most of the women a priest meets are flakes, of one kind or another. They've got to see themselves as Mary Magdalene when it isn't Joan of Arc. Why don't I ever get any Teresa of Avilas? Catherine of Siena, yes. I mean the nagging kind. Come home to Rome. Clare was a Magdalene."

"I don't understand."

"Don't try. We are talking of women. In a word, she thought her husband was running around. She came to me with the story. I knew him, I knew her, and she expects me to believe that about Larry. I tell you it gave me pause about some stories I believed in the past. She was very persuasive. If I hadn't known the two of them, particularly Larry, she might have convinced me. I wonder if she convinced Roger Dowling."

"She thought her husband had another woman?"

"She had even picked her out. Andrea Kohler. She is Larry's lawyer."

"I've met her. She's older than he is, isn't she?"

Hogan displayed his palms. "Even so, I told myself, don't be a fool. So Andrea is older than Larry, so you know Larry's views on hearth and home, marriage and fidelity. All men are sinners. Find out."

"So you called him in."

"Wrong. At least not first thing. I went to see Andrea. That, if I say so myself, was a stroke of genius. First, she is a fallen-away Catholic and this gives her a refreshing frankness. It also helped that she knew why I wanted to talk to her. 'Clare's been to see you,' she said before I was comfortable in a chair. 'I'll start with a denial. I am not now nor have I ever been engaged in alienating Larry's affections. Clare can have him as a person. I want him as a client. I have explained this to her to no avail.'" Hogan seemed to mimick Andrea Kohler when he quoted her.

"Captain, if Andrea was fooling around with Larry she would not have hesitated to tell me or anyone else. She is your basic liberated woman. When you think of incompatible people, you would have to go a far way to find a man and woman less suited for each other than Andrea and Larry. She is a former Catholic, divorced — just walked out on her family one day and entered law school — a screaming feminist. Larry is a Catholic first, last, and always. The greatest disappointment in his life is that Clare could not give him children." Hogan shook his head. "If Clare had put her mind to coming up with a basically implausible story, she could not have done better."

"What did his wife do if there were no kids?"

Hogan was nodding before he finished. "You're right. You are exactly right. But Larry would not listen. Clare should have gotten a job, if only to occupy herself, but he wouldn't hear of it. She had nothing to do. Literally. So there you are, the devil's workshop. She began to imagine a crazy world and substituted it for the real one. She had as nice a guy as you can imagine for a husband and she considered him a rat. Finally she pretended he meant to kill her."

Hogan's voice became thin as he said it, spacing the words, the remark his final indictment of Clare O'Leary.

"That was when I truly began to worry. Oh, not about the accusation, but because it exhibited such cunning. A love affair is something other people can notice; she turned to something else, something that might seem to have some basis in the real world. It was an old joke of Larry's, on the air, how he had been trying to let a contract on his wife for years and couldn't find any takers, so he might have to do the job himself. I forget how it started. Some news item, I think, and then it snowballed. He got more response on it, all of it good, because of course everyone knew it was a joke. Even the women loved it. But when Clare sat where you're sitting and tried to tell me it wasn't a joke, that Larry was dead serious, I had one of those hunches it is hard to dismiss. Anyone other than myself who heard her could begin to wonder, begin to doubt, and a whole new factor would be introduced. That crazy accusation could destroy Larry and I think she knew it."

"She wanted to destroy him?"

"Every woman wants to destroy her husband. Fifty percent

of the time, that is. Madness is just the exaggeration of something everyone has. Chesterton. Ask Roger Dowling."

Roger Dowling smiled when Phil Keegan told him of Hogan's attempt to quote Chesterton. "Dave always wanted to be an intellectual, but his sense of humor played him false. Not that humor isn't itself a sign of intelligence. But his was naturally of the slapstick kind, a mile from verbal wit." Roger Dowling puffed on his pipe and smiled beatifically through clouds of smoke. Phil Keegan had the impression that his old friend was about to fall uncharacteristically into a bout of reminiscing, recalling memories they did not share; he also suspected this was a ruse to avoid discussing Hogan's remark that someone who had not known the O'Learys would have been more easily persuaded by her story than one who did know them. Phil Keegan brought Father Dowling back to that point.

"Someone like Dave Hogan?"

"Because he knew them. The lady was a flake. His words, and he has known them both for years."

"And he is doubtless right. But as his friend Chesterton must have said, we are all a little crazy. Even you and I, Phil. Your passion is the belief that crime ought to be punished; I think it ought to be forgiven. We should be enemies, yet we're friends. Isn't that a bit crazy?"

"Neither of us has committed suicide."

"Or murder either, as far as that goes."

"It was suicide, Roger, not murder. She died from taking a bottle of sleeping pills. So she didn't leave a note. We now know she thought her husband wanted her dead. That is not good for self-esteem. She had left him, fleeing to Fox River . . ."

"Half an hour away."

Phil Keegan shrugged that aside. "A runaway doesn't even have to leave town. Remember *her* husband." He hunched a shoulder in the direction of the kitchen.

"But it is Clare's husband who refuses to accept the verdict of suicide. Did Father Hogan find that plausible, that she would kill herself?"

"I don't think anything Clare O'Leary did would have surprised him."

The conversation went on, over cribbage, and Phil Keegan drank four bottles of beer. It was the kind of evening he usually found so pleasant that the drive home to his lonely apartment was not as bad as it might be. But tonight he had the vaguely unhappy sense that he had failed to win an argument. Roger Dowling did not contest anything Hogan had said; he did not really question that Clare O'Leary's death was a suicide. But Phil Keegan found the priest oddly elusive. Had Clare O'Leary told him something neither her husband nor Father Hogan knew? It was not a thought to go to bed on.

9

CY HORVATH rose just before six in order to get in a solid hour of running before setting about preparing for his day. Jogging was a practice he had kept a secret from Keegan. Once he had shared the Captain's disdain for the dedicated runner, the kind of guy who acts as if he has found the fountain of youth in a sweaty run. It could get to you. Cy had been at it long enough to know that. A point was reached, beyond exhaustion, when you felt oddly identified with your body — the pumping knees, the gasping breath, the flab jiggling here and there — and almost separate from it, free. Your head was jostled by the jolt of your feet hitting the path, yet thought seemed clearer and more logical. Cy knew what that was like. It wasn't why he ran. He did not want to get as thick in the middle as Phil Keegan. There was little danger he would balloon up like Pianone. Fat was in Peanuts' family and not only in the head as Keegan growled. But out-of-shape is relative to shape, and Cy Horvath had been a city-wide athlete in his day, football and baseball. Like most athletes, he took the best condition he had ever been in to be normal, so it was easy to think he was out of shape. And of course if you have once been in good condition you can really fall apart when you stop exercising. He ran more of a risk than guys like Mervel, who was his age. Mervel had a beer belly and he smoked too much, but there was also the normal peril of pushing forty. You put on weight, no matter what your metabolism was. So Cy Horvath ran an hour each morning. And he was not in when Keegan called.

"Did he say what he wanted?"

Fran shook her head. The phone had wakened her but she had not gotten up. She looked sadly at her husband, puffing, wringing wet in his running clothes. Fran seemed to think his jogging was some sort of criticism of her. She had put on weight. Everyone puts on weight. But Fran had started big — not fat, big. Women had always seemed too fragile and too small before he met Fran. She didn't break when you hugged her. She could stand losing five to ten pounds, no doubt of that, but he would never say so. Running was like stopping smoking; people thought you were making big claims about your will power, or their lack of it. That was why he did not mention his jogging to Keegan.

"Where did you tell him I was?"

Fran had rolled over and pulled the covers over her shoulder. A bonus of his running was that he fixed breakfast now. Did she resent that too? "I told him you were out running around."

"He'll think I didn't come home last night."

A muffled sound of incredulity from the bed. It *was* unbelievable. Cy Horvath had married for once and all, the only kind of marriage he understood. He went down to the kitchen to call Keegan.

"You're up early," Cy said when Keegan got on the line.

"Where the hell you been?"

"Don't you know whose feast day this is?"

"Oh." Keegan obviously didn't know. Neither did Horvath. It wasn't a lie. Let Keegan think there was some Hungarian saint he didn't know about whom people like Cy Horvath were devoted to. "When you coming in, Cy?"

"I'll be there at eight. What is it?"

"It can keep. I'll see you when you get in."

Cy put on the coffee and then went to take his shower. His weariness rinsed away beneath the pelting water and he felt ten years younger. Ten years younger than he had when he dragged into the bedroom and Fran told him Keegan had called. Cy was always in before eight and Keegan knew it. Having put eggs on to boil, Cy began to cut some slices of cheese. Eggs, cheese, juice, and coffee. A helluva breakfast but, along with the running, the diet was bringing him back to the condition he had enjoyed when he had been all-city tackle. He was sure Keegan wanted to talk about Clare O'Leary.

This guess had become a conviction by the time he was driving downtown. It was the Father Dowling connection. The priest always knew as much as they did about anything under investigation, for the simple reason that Keegan kept him informed. Which was all right with Cy Horvath, since Roger Dowling was an old friend of Keegan's, the kind of priest Cy considered the right kind, and he had often been of help. Nor did it hurt that Cy sensed the priest thought pretty highly of him. The added factor in the Clare O'Leary case was that the woman had gone to see Roger Dowling shortly before she died. Maybe the pastor of St. Hilary's had given Keegan something they didn't already know, something that changed the look of the thing.

Cy Horvath was not sure Clare O'Leary had committed suicide. He didn't doubt the official verdict exactly, he just did not accept it. Maybe he would simply have left it there if it had not been for Agnes Lamb. Agnes had kept on the Clare O'Leary matter as if it were still a wide-open investigation. If nothing else, she had turned up interesting things about the Stagecoach Inn.

"You find me someplace where you can't buy it, I'll whistle Dixie, but that place is crawling with it. I talked with the maids and they know. Cleaning up rooms, you learn a lot. It's not just that someone has a joint from time to time. Some of those rooms reek. There are other things too, papers, plastic bags, the sort of thing they have seen too much of already. And I don't have to tell you what they think, Horvath. Here's whitey doing whatever he likes in that nice motel, but let one of us try anything, and whammo."

Agnes tapped ashes from the tip of her cigarette. "That is a line of thought I don't encourage. I know lots of blacks who are getting away with at least as much. That's not the point. The point is that that motel is one weird place, so what is a supposedly nice lady like Clare O'Leary doing there?"

The clientele of the Stagecoach was for the most part nomadic; people came and went and were never heard from again, but that is generally true with motels and hotels. There was a recurrent minority, however, and this was not restricted to salesmen. Some of those ladies who hung around the Billet-Doux were repeaters.

"The profile is a lot like the O'Leary woman. The farthest away any of that bunch comes from is a hundred miles. Driving here from Waukegan is not as ridiculous as it sounds."

"Was Mrs. O'Leary a repeater?"

"I wish I knew. I checked the register. Nothing. Ganser denies it, the maids don't know. That piano-player, Twinkie, puts on a retarded act whenever I try to get anything out of him. None of the staff gives any reason to doubt she came just that once and killed herself. There is still a woman named Hilda I must talk to. She normally oversees the wing of the motel Mrs. O'Leary stayed in and she was on duty when she checked in. She had to go out of town but when she comes back..."

"How do you know that?"

"Ganser. She called in."

"Where did she go out of town?"

"Lieutenant, it's a straw, that's all. I don't imagine she'll know any more than the rest of them about Clare O'Leary."

"Find out. And forget about Ganser."

God, she was touchy. Anything that sounded like criticism made Agnes bristle. Well, who knows what it's like to be black? Cy didn't. It was hard enough being Hungarian, or it had been when he was growing up, and not even his athletic accomplishments entirely erased the difficulty. He assured Agnes it was just routine and he spared her the little lecture on routine. It was Keegan's and they all knew it by heart.

Had Keegan heard of that and called him in to read him out? It was not routine to go on investigating a death after it had been officially declared a suicide.

Keegan sat behind his desk, coat off, cigar lit and half gone; he had the air of someone who had been at his desk for hours. He looked up impatiently at Horvath. "Clare O'Leary," he said without preliminary. "What the hell do we really know about her except that Phelps said she died of an overdose of sleeping pills?"

"Not much," Cy answered before settling into a chair. They knew she had come to Fox River, checked into the Stagecoach, apparently looked up Roger Dowling's address in the book...

"She didn't write the phone number too, did she?"

"Just the address. The handwriting was hers. Why the phone number when she apparently didn't call the rectory but went on over there? Don't know. And we don't know what she said to him. Do we?"

Keegan shook his head. "Only that it wasn't anything we don't know from other sources."

Horvath smiled. That was like Dowling. There were times when Horvath was sure the pastor of St. Hilary's was pulling their leg but Keegan probably would not like to have such a suspicion voiced.

"And we have been told quite a lot by the husband."

That was when Keegan took over and, as Horvath had suspected, it was the visit to Waukegan that still lingered. "The husband doesn't think she committed suicide. Neither does the lady lawyer. And O'Leary's friend Father Hogan isn't too convinced either. When you put all that up against Phelps, it makes you wonder. It makes me wonder, anyway. I started thinking of it last night and hardly got to sleep. I was at this desk at six o'clock and I don't know any more now than I did. You and Agnes have gone ahead with this, haven't you?"

"Just routine."

"Sure. Tell me what you've found out."

Whatever Keegan expected, he was clearly disappointed with what Cy could offer him. Agnes had found out that the Stagecoach Inn and a number of other motels in the vicinity were places where drugs could be had. Keegan and Horvath had known this for years and it was a thorn in the side. But how do you tell an eager young cop that evidence of a crime is not always enough. Lamb also thought there was a link between the motel drug traffic and the death of Clare O'Leary.

"How do you mean?" Keegan traced the short thrust of his nose with the knuckle of his thumb. It went without saying that drugs were at the center of most of the problems they faced now, no matter how far a radius might be drawn from that center. With such certainty they should have been able to clean up the area in a matter of weeks. They could have, too, but the center was a protected one, and even the protection was protected, so that it was difficult to know where exactly things went wrong when an investigation or a prosecution that had seemed assured of success suddenly went kaput. They had their suspicions, of course, many of them pointing to the Pianones on the city council and thus indirectly to Peanuts, the Pianone whose presence on the force was a source of either amusement or indignation, depending on your mood; and to Robertson, the chief, whose appointment was political and whose masters thus numbered among them the Pianones. And there were people in the prosecutor's office whose crusading spirit dimmed on occasion. None of this came within a rocket shot of admissible evidence, but not everything known for sure is provable. So Keegan listened to what Agnes had turned up at the Stagecoach and Horvath did not blame him if he did not enjoy hearing about things that should have been wiped out long ago. Keegan was more interested in the fact that quite a number of those middle-aged females were regulars at the Stagecoach.

"What's the big attraction? Don't tell me they're all hopheads?"

"If Agnes is right, they get a little grass without trouble. Believe it or not, the attraction appears to be the big guy who plays piano there."

"Twinkie Zeugner?"

"Can you imagine anyone daring to call a man that size Twinkie?"

"He seems to like it. Look, Cy, none of this matters unless Clare O'Leary was a regular there, and that's ruled out. If she had died of a drug overdose, that would..." Keegan stopped. "Where's the autopsy report?"

"I already checked it, Captain. Sleeping pills. That's all they mentioned."

"How much you want to bet that's all they looked for? They were told the body had been found with an empty bottle of sleeping pills on the table beside the bed."

"They say they gave it the full treatment."

"I'm going to demand proof of that," Keegan growled.

"Good idea."

"Either one would do, Cy: that she had been there before, or that she was somehow linked with whatever's going on there in drugs. Without that, we have nothing but the insistence of her husband that she did not commit suicide."

Cy got to his feet. "I'll see what we can find out."

"We?"

"Agnes Lamb. Is that okay?"

"If you think she can be of help."

"There's no doubt about that."

When would Keegan just accept the fact that Agnes Lamb was a good cop?

Keegan sent for Lamb and while they waited for her, went on about the O'Leary woman. "Why is everyone so damned sure they know who is and who is not suicidal? My theory is that it comes as a surprise to the one who does it. One way or another, she is dead, and if it wasn't suicide, it had to be an accident or someone shoved all those pills down her throat or we don't trust Phelps. It's too bad. I really wish we could give O'Leary reason to think she hadn't done it. A different sort of guy would be relieved at the official finding. I told you she had accused him of wanting to kill her?"

Cy's watch was concealed by the cuff of his shirt and he didn't want to check the time in an obvious way. Keegan's hope that he had overlooked something was not surviving this exchange, but that didn't mean he would drop it. If Cy knew him, Keegan would now want to start on a painful and chronological review of the death of Clare O'Leary. He was saved that by Agnes Lamb's entry.

Keegan was startled to have Lamb just burst in on him, but it was Horvath she addressed.

"That woman Hilda? The one who worked at the Stagecoach they said went out of town?" Agnes paused and took a steady breath. "She went out of town all right. She's been in the Cook County morgue for the past five days."

10

THERE was a blonde at the piano bar, an unlit cigarette in the fingers of one hand, the stem of her martini glass in those of the other, her lidded eyes fixed significantly on Twinkie Zeugner while he played "Danny Boy." Twinkie knew the type. She would do better to enjoy her cigarette or her drink or both. It was an old trick, the passionate stare meant to establish a special rapport with the man behind the piano. Twinkie returned the soulful look. What the hell, it was his job, but if the blonde thought it meant anything beyond this set or at any rate beyond the Billet-Doux, she was going to be disappointed. What he didn't like was that her hair reminded him of Clare O'Leary.

That was ridiculous. For one thing, Clare had not gotten her blondness from a bottle. For another, she did not moon over Twinkie, which is why he had found her attractive. She was a relief from the others. The first time he asked if he could sit with her he thought she was going to turn him down. In the Billet-Doux, that would have been a switch. When he asked what she would like to hear and she said whatever he liked, Twinkie was a little put out. He must be getting spoiled. What the hell, he knew the Billet-Doux was not the real world nor were the women who fawned over him there much to look at in the light of day. Clare O'Leary didn't belong, and that is what fascinated him about her. That is why he pursued her and not vice versa. It felt good. He felt like a man again. The first time he asked her to stop by his room, he hoped she wouldn't, but she went on surprising him. He expected her to be shocked when he offered her some grass but she lit up without hesitation.

"I've always wondered what it was like."

"You've never tried it before?" He wanted to take the joint out of her hand. It was like taking her virginity. But he didn't stop her. Junkies love company. She tried coke too once or twice, but mainly she was satisfied with grass.

Thinking of her now, knowing he would never see her again, he played tunes like "Danny Boy" and that was all right with customers. No one objects to crying in their beer a bit and it is no accident that sentimental ballads are popular in bars. But Twinkie was playing these for himself, and with feeling. Wilma was there too, a shadowy figure at a table near the door. He had announced that this tune was for her and the blonde had asked, "Who's Billy?"

"Billet-Doux," Twinkie said and got a laugh. That made it necessary for him to chord into the mood he wanted and then he had them because he had himself; that was the real secret of entertainment, and he could almost feel what the tune was doing to Wilma back there in the dark, knowing he was playing it for her. No matter that he called her Billy.

Wilma was nervous as a cat because of the time the black cop had been spending in the motel.

"She's been talking to every maid here," Wilma said. "I thought they said it was suicide. Why don't they let us alone?"

"She talk to you again?"

"No! God forbid. The maids."

Well, they wouldn't be talking to Hilda, Twinkie thought. He had heard Ganser tell the cop Hilda had phoned in to say she was called out of town. Ganser thought her daughter was having a baby, he didn't know. The cop let it go by and Twinkie couldn't believe it. Anyone could see Ganser was lying. Hilda had no daughter and Ganser knew it. Twinkie would bet Hilda hadn't called in and if Ganser said she had, that meant they wanted to be rid of her. Temporarily? It was possible. But days passed and

Hilda had not returned. The black cop did, and she had not forgotten Hilda. It would only be a matter of time before the lid
blew off and Twinkie wasn't positive he was sorry about it. Unless Lamb, the black cop, gave it up. Somehow Twinkie didn't
think she would. Neither did Wilma.

"She's bound to find out about all the stuff available in this
place."

"Why, Wilma, I thought you were saving yourself for me."

"Don't be a jerk. I mean the grass and coke and whatever
the hell else is bought and sold all over this motel."

Twinkie reached over and put his finger to her lips and shook
his head. "Think it if you have to but don't say it, sweetheart. You
want to stay on the Stagecoach circuit, mum's the word, okay?
You don't know nothing. That is what Mr. Maxwell would expect
of his employees."

"If she hasn't found out already, she will."

"So what?"

"She's a cop!"

"Right. Which means that what's going on here isn't going to
surprise her at all. This sort of thing interests police only around
election time. Meaning that, beyond the police, you take care of
the politicians. Now, if you think Maxwell hasn't covered his bets
any better than that, you can lift your weight in wheat germ. Relax, Wilma. What's the point of getting your body in the pink if
you're going to be a worrywart?"

"I'll stop worrying when the police stop hanging around."

It made him wonder what Wilma's real worry was. Maxwell
had something on everyone who worked for him; he called it em-
ployee insurance. If there wasn't something before he took you
on, he made sure there was pretty soon or you were on your way.
Twinkie just hoped his confidence in Maxwell was well placed.
He had kept out of trouble so far working for Maxwell and that
track record was good enough for him. Still, when you thought
about it, there were reasons to get a little jumpy. Clare O'Leary
being found dead in bed was bad enough, without cops running

around the place all week. He really didn't blame Wilma for being
nervous. Who can relax with a cop in the house? Wilma maybe
didn't know how much reason they all had to worry, and if she
didn't know she wasn't going to learn it from Twinkie Zeugner.
You put a cop like that Lamb dame on a scent and she might turn
up more than Maxwell paid to keep quiet. But it was best not to
dwell on these things. It could make you wonder about the verdict
of suicide on Clare.

Twinkie would have gone on not quite entertaining these
thoughts and feeling affectionate condescension for Wilma if
Maxwell himself had not shown up. Ganser took Twinkie into the
sauna to tell him. A bead of sweat formed on the bridge of the
manager's nose and worked its way down to the tip while Twinkie
insisted on getting the message straight.

"What room's he in?"

"He's not staying here, Twinkie. That wouldn't make much
sense right now, would it?" Ganser seemed to be balancing the
bead of sweat. "He's downtown at the High-Rise."

"You seen him?"

The drop of sweat flew free when Ganser shook his head.
"The call just came. He wants to see you."

"Someone called up and said this is Maxwell and I want to
see Zeugner?"

"'I want to see Twinkie,'" Ganser corrected. "Don't worry,
it was him."

"Maxwell himself make the call?"

"He came on after I answered."

"Someone else spoke first?"

Ganser thought about it. Twinkie did not like this. He was
never happy about seeing Maxwell. In the same room with Maxwell, Twinkie was reminded of their first meeting, when he had
been free. Now he was a slave. A happy slave, and that made it
worse. There were pictures of Twinkie at two, even three years
old, walking, with a pacifier stuck in his mouth. He couldn't remember the thing himself but his folks kidded him about it later.

He had to be weaned from a goddamn rubber tit. Well, he was beyond weaning now and Maxwell controlled the pacifiers. It wasn't really because he doubted Ganser that he went on about the phone call. Actually, it sounded just like Maxwell; that was his trademark. But why the High-Rise Hotel in downtown Fox River? That suggested more than caution. Nobody was going to have any problem establishing a connection between Maxwell and the Stagecoach. He wasn't staying away to keep the fact he owned it secret. So why the games?

"Jesus, Twinkie, you think I'm going to ask him a question like that? I'm just passing on the message, okay? You want to leave Maxwell downtown cooling his heels, lots of luck." Ganser wiped the tip of his nose and grabbed the handle of the sauna door.

"You got any messages for Maxwell, Ganser?"

"Yeah. Tell him to get the cops off our backs."

"I'll pass on your complaint."

"Complaint?" Ganser let go of the door. "Who's complaining? I figure Maxwell will want to know about those cops."

"So he can stay at the High-Rise rather than here?"

Ganser looked up at him. "Don't be a shit, Zeugner. I cover for you all the time."

"Call me Twinkie." He said it with a solemn expression and Ganser didn't know what to make of it, so he left. Twinkie felt pretty cheap. That's the way it worked. Maxwell could kick him around, so he took it out on Ganser. A whole theory of human nature seemed to be lurking in the wings, but he had to step on it. He didn't want to keep Max waiting.

The man who opened the door of Maxwell's suite at the High-Rise stared at Twinkie as if his optic nerves were dead. Twinkie had a sudden thought of purgatory. Make it hell. This goon would kill, maim, or applaud Twinkie without even having to change gears. Going past him, Twinkie knew how average-sized guys felt around him. The doorkeeper was a head taller than Twinkie and he seemed to have an umpire's chest protector on under his coat.

The room had a Miami Beach look, which was one way to handle the Illinois winters. Pale green deep shag rug, glass-top tables, couches, and chairs off-white. Maxwell sat on the center cushion of one of the couches and the broad welcoming smile on his tanned face was somehow more menacing than the lost soul who opened the door. Maxwell was wearing Florida clothes too: his slacks and sports coat two shades of light brown, a lime green shirt open at the neck. Maxwell shook hands sitting down, like royalty, like Twinkie himself when he received fans at the piano.

"Twinkie, I think you've finally stopped growing. I knew this lug when he was under six foot." This lie was addressed to the redhead curled up in the corner of another couch, wearing some sort of silky lounge suit and a petulant expression.

"This the guy we flew all the way from Florida to see?"

"Go powder your nose, Jill. Have a drink. We lost an hour coming up."

"I don't want a drink."

"Then take a nap. Scoot."

Twinkie suspected Jill's days were numbered. Maxwell might leave her up north when he went back to Florida if she didn't act like a wound-up doll. Maxwell had been watching Twinkie watch Jill go. "It's my weakness, Twinkie. There'll always be more where she came from. That's what's so wonderful. I can never run out of them. It's a vice you don't have, I know, and I admire you for it. Smoke a cigarette if you want."

So Maxwell set the scene right there: Twinkie was a coke-head and there was no comparison between that and using up girls as if they were rental equipment. Maxwell waved him to a chair. Up close you could see the wrinkles in the corners of Max's eyes. There was something wrong with his optic nerves too. "Why did you have to spoil your record, Twinkie?"

"Tell me about it."

"Clare O'Leary."

There was no point in trying to engage Maxwell in a staring match, as Twinkie should have known, but he gave it a try. In maybe fifteen seconds he looked away. "It wasn't anything serious."

"Tell that to her husband."

Twinkie did light up a cigarette then. He could feel his underarms grow moist and he never sweated. "We made it a couple times. That was all. That's never been a rule, Max. The opposite is. I'm supposed to keep the customers happy."

"Dead isn't happy."

"I don't know anything about that. She committed suicide."

"Twinkie, I want you to get away for a while. Come back to Florida with me. You can have Jill. What the hell, maybe it's time for you to retire."

"Whatever you say, Max. You own a club in Florida or what?"

He knew Maxwell's business interests did not extend that far. Suddenly he felt perfectly calm. He was scared to death, yet he was calm. Twinkie had never heard of anyone retiring from Maxwell's operations and, as for a pension, he was as likely to get that as Jill. He had shown interest in a girl for a change and Max would never give him anything he wanted. Maxwell considered Twinkie to be dumb and that misunderstanding was his main weapon now. Max had to think Twinkie believed this bullshit about retirement. If Max wanted to get rid of him he would have something more permanent in mind. Had the ghoul at the door looked at him with anticipation? Twinkie could believe it. Every road has an end, but he didn't think he was all that far along on his. Max had other ideas, that was clear. So Twinkie sat there, joking about Florida and lying about the good times he and Maxwell had shared. One thing was sure. He had seen the last of the Stagecoach Inn. He couldn't go back there now, not even to pick up his things. If he got a chance to go anywhere, that is.

"Finish the week, what the hell. The damage is done. Let's say Monday you're on your way. I'll give you the name of my hotel. We'll get your new life started right."

How easily he might have believed Maxwell. He wanted to believe him so bad it hurt.

He was allowed to go, finally, but not, as it happened, alone. After the elevator doors closed on him he punched the mezzanine button and it was from there, looking over the railing, that he saw old deadeye come out of an elevator and hurry across the lobby. Twinkie stayed right where he was. He settled into a chair that seemed more of a prop than anything; he might have been the first one to sit in it. Five minutes later the ghoul came back, and his expression was even grimmer when he retraced his steps to the elevator.

Twinkie went down to the desk and registered. "Call me immediately if the airline finds my luggage."

"Yes, sir." The clerk scanned the card. "Mr. O'Toole. You won't be needing a bellboy now, will you?"

In his room, Twinkie looked up a number and dialed it.

"Agnes Lamb, please. I'd like to speak with Officer Agnes Lamb."

11

"I'll tell you one thing, Roger," Phil Keegan said. "Phelps can take suicide and stick it in his ear. The O'Leary case is open again as far as I'm concerned."

"You think she was killed?"

"I think she didn't commit suicide. No more than the maid Hilda did."

Phil continued draining his beer glass but his eye was on Roger Dowling. He put down the glass with a bang. "Bodies are piling up in this damned town and I don't like it."

Roger smiled at his old friend's hyperbole. "What was the cause of Hilda Johnson's death?"

"The way it looks, she was pretty well smashed and she drove her car into her garage and left the motor running. She lived alone and the body wasn't discovered for days. What is suspicious about a car parked in a garage after it burns up all the gas in the tank?"

"An accident?"

"I said it looks that way, not that it is. I talked with O'Leary not an hour ago and you can imagine his reaction." Roger Dowling did not like his own reaction to Phil Keegan's obvious pleasure that he was now able to offer Clare's widower some basis for his conviction that his wife had not committed suicide. He might have shared Phil's satisfaction if he could rid his memory of the image of Clare O'Leary sitting where Phil now did and telling him her husband was having an affair with another woman and threatened to kill her. Was murder preferable to suicide?

He had not been able to avoid talking with Dave Hogan. The Waukegan pastor made a special trip to Fox River so that he could discover how Dowling had reacted to Clare's story.

"I had no reason to doubt her."

Hogan smiled as if he had just guessed the right answer. "Even you. I've had a little bet with myself that she wouldn't have been able to fool you, but obviously she did."

"How much did you bet?"

"Nothing. It was just a bet."

Hogan was hard to get off the topic of Clare and Larry O'Leary, obviously eager for Roger Dowling to see the couple exactly as he had. Larry was the long-suffering husband, Clare the flaky wife. "Did you hear about the will, Roger?"

"No, I haven't."

Hogan slid forward on his chair. "Listen to this. It will give you a sense of the man. What he planned to do with his money, on the assumption that he would die before Clare, was first to provide for her needs as long as she lived and then the Clare O'Leary Foundation would go into operation. Well, now that Clare's dead, he's going ahead with it right now. He is going to sink all but a sliver of his money into a foundation named for his wife and devote most of his time to administering it. Andrea Kohler worked night and day on it and it's all ironed out." Hogan sat back. "This is the man who wanted to kill his wife? This is the lawyer he was having an affair with. Baloney. Don't get me wrong, Roger. She could have fooled me too if I didn't know what I know. First thing Larry wants to do is make a donation to the Poor Clares. I think that is very touching."

Roger Dowling managed not to reveal his own reaction. He told himself it was injured pride he felt, but that only worked if Clare O'Leary had been lying. It was getting very difficult to believe she had been telling the truth.

And now Phil Keegan had turned into another champion of Larry O'Leary.

"Phil, if her death was not due to suicide and you are seriously pursuing the possibility that it was murder, who are your suspects?"

"Good question. The more we learn about the Stagecoach Inn, the more obvious it is that she could not have chosen a worse place to take a room. That motel is a regular drug store. And there's something else. There may have been something going on between Mrs. O'Leary and the guy who plays the piano in the lounge down there. Twinkie Zeugner." Keegan waited but Roger Dowling did not react. "We discounted this because half the women staying there have crushes on Zeugner."

"Twinkie?"

"Don't ask me. He's a giant. Looks like a football player."

"Phil, I cannot believe I could be so wrong about a person. Have you talked with Twinkie Zeugner?"

"We've talked with him several times, but not since the phone call."

"The phone call?"

"Telling us to ask Zeugner what was going on between him and Clare O'Leary."

"I'd like to be there when you talk to him."

"Sure."

"What's his motive supposed to be?"

"He may have had nothing to do with her death, Roger. But he knows more than he told us. They all know more than they told us. We wouldn't know what we do if Cy and Agnes hadn't hung in there. Maxwell has got connections, here, in Chicago. Don't ask me to prove it, but I know. There wouldn't be the traffic at the Stagecoach if Maxwell weren't cleared all up and down the line."

"If there are drugs out there, why don't you make an arrest?"

Keegan sighed. "The rules of evidence, among other things. Things like a lack of enthusiasm in the prosecutor's office. Besides, that doesn't seem to be the reason why women like Clare O'Leary hang around the place."

"Why do women go there?"

"Twinkie Zeugner."

"He sounds like a gold mine."

But it was difficult to imagine Clare O'Leary developing a schoolgirl crush on a nightclub entertainer. Even if she had, what would it have had to do with her death? Twinkie Zeugner might be a lady-killer but was he a Bluebeard? Grant that she had been overcome by infatuation, could this explain her death, whether by her own hand or another's? That simply made no sense. But suicide made no sense either. On that score, Roger Dowling was prepared to be more adamant than Larry O'Leary himself.

He sat on in the study thinking after Phil left. The woman who had come to him, who fled Waukegan in order to save her life, did not come to Fox River in order to take it. Another puzzle was the death of the maid Hilda Johnson, who had been in charge of the section of the motel in which Clare's room was located.

Father Dowling let his pipe die out because the tip of his tongue was raw; he was less reconciled to what was thought to have happened to Clare O'Leary than before. He picked up his breviary and read Compline distractedly. *Nunc dimittis servum tuum, domine, in pace*: "Now dismiss thy servant in peace, O Lord." Peace! When he closed the book, he offered up a prayer for the repose of the soul of Clare O'Leary. Her husband would have Masses in abundance said for her, still more proof, according to Hogan, that the grief-stricken widower had been devoted to his wife in her lifetime too. Dave Hogan said Clare O'Leary could have fooled him. Roger Dowling wondered if Larry O'Leary had actually done so.

He had not yet gone upstairs when the phone rang. He picked it up quickly lest it waken Mrs. Murkin, but as he put the instrument to his ear he heard the familiar click of the housekeeper's phone being picked up.

"Saint Hilary's rectory, Father Dowling speaking."

"Father, you don't know me, but I'd like to talk with you."
Roger Dowling glanced at his watch. It was going on one in the morning. "Of course. You mean right away?"
"If it's possible, Father."
"I assume it's important."
"Aren't you the priest Clare O'Leary came to see?"
"Are you Twinkie Zeugner?"
"How did you know that?"
"Just a guess. I'll put the porch light on so you won't have trouble finding the place."
"How did you know I was calling you?"
Roger Dowling could have bitten his tongue for voicing his hunch as to the identity of this caller; because of all those pipefuls of tobacco, he felt as if he already had. He sensed it would be best to be frank with Zeugner. Mentioning his name had brought a note of wariness into the man's voice. From husky confidential it had become wobbly and remote. He told Twinkie of the phone call the police had received.
"Heyzoo Christmas. He's not wasting any time. Father, I'm being set up."
"Come here and we'll talk about it."
"No. The police could be watching your house."
"Why on earth would they do that?"
"I don't know. Why would someone call and tell them to talk to me about Clare O'Leary?"
"If you're at the Stagecoach, you are in far more danger of encountering the police than if you came here."
"I'm not there."
"I see. I'll come to you, then. Where are you?"
For a moment Roger Dowling was certain Zeugner was not going to tell him. He half expected to hear the receiver being put down.
"I'm at the High-Rise. Downtown. Do you know it?"
"Yes."

"Don't ask for me at the desk. Come right up to 1162. Knock and call out for Mr. O'Toole."

"I'll be there directly."

He waited for the sound of a phone being put down, then said, "Hang up, Marie."

"You can't go down there, Father. Should I call Captain Keegan?"

"Only if you want to start looking around for a nice nursing home."

12

LARRY's capacity for self-deception was, Andrea Kohler reflected, a prerequisite of his job. It took a lot of imagination to regard his essentially modest spot at WKIS as the very center of Show Business. But Larry did think of himself as a peer of the legendary stars of stage, screen, and radio, as he inevitably put it. His programs had, admittedly, extended Larry's fame to the very outer fringes of the signal's reach. Whether to be known by twenty million people rather than only twenty adds anything other than a quantitative difference to fame was one of the questions Larry was welcome to discuss with Father Hogan while swilling imported Guinness in bottles before the rectory fire. To be big in Waukegan is to be small, and Larry should be man enough to face up to that. Of course he wasn't. Or maybe it was because he was a man that he had such an imperfect grasp of reality.

If he could be deceived about himself, it was perhaps in the cards he could deceive himself about his feelings for Clare. Despite his jabber on the air, he could never really say anything against her. It was an aspect of his self-esteem. How could Larry O'Leary possibly have had a wife who despised him? It boggled the mind. Ergo, Clare must, despite appearances, love Larry, and Larry, being Larry, must return her love. Pure fantasy. But it got worse after Clare was dead and buried. Larry was obviously casting himself for the role of the most disconsolate widower of all time. His revelation of the provisions of his will, particularly the projected Clare O'Leary Foundation, came as a revelation to his lawyer. Andrea had never heard of any of this, but there was the story in the Waukegan paper and, as Larry told her when she phoned him about it, the story was being picked up by other papers around the state.

"If you want to redraft your will, I wish you would contact me directly, not via the newspapers."

"What do you mean?" He sounded genuinely baffled. Doubtless he was.

"When can we get together to rewrite your will, Larry?"

"I suppose the establishment of the Clare O'Leary Foundation will have to be redescribed."

"Described, Larry. I never heard of it before."

"I'm certain we spoke of it. In any case, there is no need to wait. I would like to set it up immediately. I have a number of projects I want to get going on right away."

Andrea set it up.

She knew nothing of tax-free foundations, and Illinois law proved to be deliciously complicated. As her research continued, she found herself conceding that Larry had indeed hit upon a most uncannily attractive tax dodge. The two of them would be officers of the trust endowment and could write off the bulk of their expenses against the Foundation and drain the thing by means of huge salaries when the time for that become opportune. Larry's purported naiveté must mask a shrewdness whose depths she was only beginning to suspect. Even the seemingly idiotic publicity, just blurting out the idea and having it spread across the papers, seemed a display of cunning. The IRS were going to think they too had been in on this from the beginning. When a taxpayer ties his hands in public, the tax collector can scarcely suspect him of duplicity. "I think of it as something like a vow of poverty. Sell all that you have and give the proceeds to the poor. Isn't that what we're told to do? This is my vow of poverty. I am tying up all my worldly goods so that I can turn them to goals my wife would have approved of. I don't lay any claim to be a Franciscan..."

Hell no, he didn't. Let the interviewer and then the reader do it for him. Andrea did not understand Larry's attitude toward religion any more than she had his attitude toward Clare. It must be clear to everyone other than himself that he exploited it, turning it to his own purposes, making religious belief a sort of tribal affair that called for loyalty and passing it on. When she thought of it, Andrea found Larry's ability to dissociate himself from reality almost at will frightening. What did he really think of her? Did he admit even in the privacy of his own mind that they had been in bed together, that it had been great, and that afterward he had sobbed and said he had never realized love could be so wonderful? His remark made Andrea see their relationship as it really was. She had not escaped New Berlin by kidding herself.

Okay, truth time. It was nice to have a younger man, even one as unprepossessing as Larry O'Leary, unprepossessing by comparison with Jack, that is, for her lover. It was flattering. One of the chilling realities of breaking free from domestic security was the realization that all those flirty flirty men who had seemed to be three deep at suburban parties faded into nothingness when a woman was free and in principle open to persuasion. If Andrea had felt invisible as a wife and mother, she began to see how bad invisibility could really be for the unattached middle-aged woman. Maybe if she had hung around bars, like Clare, it would have been different. But in the ordinary course of her day she was safe as a nun in a retreat house for fairies. Which does damaging things to a woman's sense of pride. So the truth was that she had needed Larry's attention when he turned it on her and she was receptive to his fumbling sensuality. He obviously expected to be repulsed. None of this made her less successful as a lawyer or took away ground she had gained since her liberation.

One day the phone rang and when she answered it she was startled to hear the voice of Jack, Junior.

"Are you calling from Tampa?"

"I've been in Chicago nearly two weeks, on business. I've been reading about you in the paper."

"Nothing bad, I hope."

"So do I."

He paused and Andrea said nothing, closing her eyes, making her mouth a straight line as maternal affection drained from her. She could hear Jack's voice in her son's and with it the old note of accusation.

He said, "Your client who is about to outdo Saint Francis by making most of his assets tax free..."

"That was in the Chicago paper?"

"No. I read it in the Waukegan *Flash* or whatever it is."

"Why on earth would you read a Waukegan paper?"

"To check up on my mother. It worked. You figure prominently in a story guaranteed to bring a lump to any reader's throat."

"How is everything in Florida?"

"Flourishing."

"Your father too?"

"Oh, yes. In his fashion. He is afflicted with good taste and that somewhat limits his range of opportunities. No girl friends, no hanky-panky with the spouses of clients, no headlines in the Waukegan *Washcloth*."

"You've been drinking."

"Correction. I am drinking. I am toasting your client in fermented crocodile tears. Do the two of you have plans?

"I'm not sure I'd want to have this conversation with you sober, Jack. I certainly don't want it in your present condition."

"Didn't she leave a note accusing you of breaking up her happy home?"

Andrea hung up the phone. When her anger subsided she thought how eerie it was to have her son hanging around Waukegan, apparently spying on her. Eerie? It was awful. But she did not know what she could do to stop him.

13

MERVEL watched with one eye, the better to focus, the seven minutes Bruce Wiggins devoted to what he called the Canute of Waukegan. Perhaps he meant Croesus. Wiggins spoke in hushed and reverent tones of the man whose wife had been found dead in a Fox River motel and who had now decided to distribute his wealth in honor of his departed wife. Compassion mixed with sincerity on Wiggins's face, and it was clear to the viewer that he too was a potential *Poverello*.

What is the romantic attraction of poverty to the affluent, Mervel wondered, punching the off button on his remote controls and reaching for his drink. It must sound like an absence of care, a getting rid of all the things and pressures weighing upon us. An odd thought that the freedom of the poor was something other than deprivation. But then there was voluntary poverty, the vow, the religious ideal, and it was some version of this Bruce Wiggins was attributing to Larry O'Leary of Waukegan, apparently taking his cue from O'Leary himself.

Mervel drank deep but his resentment did not cool as did the tube of his black and white Japanese-made seven-inch concession to television. If O'Leary himself was not in television he was in the next worst thing, and this effort to tout him as a latter-day Franciscan smacked of collusion. Mervel's normal reportorial skepticism was magnified by the fact that the enemy was involved. Wiggins, he was sure, would not know an altruistic act if he met one, and O'Leary was incapable of committing one. Whence came these convictions? Partly from booze, no doubt, partly from revulsion for the make-believe reporters of TV news. Partly, finally, from the fruit of experience: goodness is rare. The odds that things in Waukegan were as Wiggins portrayed them were from slim to non-existent. So what? If he were right — and doubt did not enter into it — he had a professional opportunity to expose the hollowness and mendacity of television news coverage.

Mervel stirred in the easy chair that was an eyesore, but in every other way comfortable. The cushion had gone the way of all fabric and had been replaced by two layers of foam rubber cut more or less to size. The point was not looks but to make the chair as comfortable as possible.

To drink *chez lui* as opposed to elsewhere was undertaken with the notion that the desired objective was oblivion. He had had an indeterminate number of drinks since settling in for the night and the thoughts generated by Wiggins on the screen led on to other thoughts that could be pursued only with a relatively sober mind. Absentmindedly he drank what was left in the glass beside him. He had difficulty getting out of the chair, but that was as much a feature of its comfort as of his condition. Coffee. He had read that the sobering effects of coffee were a myth. In his case, it was a myth that worked. His head cleared slightly at the aroma that greeted him when he opened the coffee can, and once the smell of brewing coffee filled the apartment Mervel was on the way to recovery.

It was late, after midnight, but he did not hesitate to dial the number he found written in fading pencil in his address book. He was answered before the second ring was complete.

"Tuttle and Tuttle," a querulous voice said.

"You're up."

"We never close."

"With your sort of client, I'm not surprised."

"Is that you, Governor."

"Mervel."

"What the hell are you calling at this hour of the night for?"

"I know it's early, Tuttle, but I need some information about legal matters."

"I don't handle paternity suits."

"You gonna be in your office a while longer?"

"I can be. Bring a six-pack."

First he had two cups of near scalding coffee. In the bathroom he began to make preparations for shaving, then stopped himself. So he wasn't completely sober. He did have a morning feeling and that was the next best thing. Clarity of mind did not bring regret that he had called Tuttle. The kind of information he wanted required the semi-crook Tuttle was. There were lawyers who would roundly deny that the laws of Illinois were manipulable in the manner Mervel was betting on. Nor did Tuttle disappoint him.

"Let me get this straight." Tuttle did not refer to the Irish woolen hat worn low over his eyes even inside. "Your friend wants to get his money where the IRS can't touch it. There are many ways."

"Legal ways?"

"Sir," Tuttle chided. "I shall begin with those. Does he have a Keogh plan?"

"What's that?"

"A retirement plan for the self-employed. Is your friend self-employed?"

Mervel hesitated. "What if he weren't?"

Tuttle tipped his hat back. "Mervel, a suggestion. Let us get rid of your imaginary friend so we can talk more freely. That is the oldest trick in the book, like the man who asks the doctor about clap because his friend has it. What are you up to, Mervel?"

"I want to start a foundation under the laws of Illinois. Call it the Tuttle Foundation. Into it I want to put everything I've got. Does this make any sense?"

"There already is a Tuttle Foundation."

"You're kidding."

"Named for my dear father. Alas, it does not have the endowment I had hoped. Still, as a legal instrument, it is there when the time comes."

"What's the advantage?"

"For you?"

"For anybody?"

Tuttle crushed an empty beer can and sent it soaring toward the wastepaper basket in the corner. He missed and the can made quite a racket. There was a muted knock on the wall behind Tuttle. He pounded back. "You are thinking about this guy in Waukegan, aren't you? I think we may have had the same thought. Mervel, have you any idea how many private foundations there are?"

"Ford, Rockefeller, Guggenheim.... A dozen? Two dozen?"

"There are thousands. It takes volumes to list them all. They are of every conceivable size and set up for any number of purposes. They represent the philanthropy our tax laws encourage. If you can't keep your money and either you or Uncle Sam must choose how it is to be given away, well, you can see the attraction."

"A choice of weapons."

"But dead either way? Not necessarily. Not necessarily at all. For one thing, there is the skim. Welfare, philanthropy, charities, disease drives, you name it, they all involve a skim. Congress sets up some welfare program and what happens? A huge number of jobs are created that pay fifty to sixty thousand, well above what are alleged to be comparable civilian jobs, and they are filled with idiots who could not make a fraction of that amount on the open market. Politicians bleed for the poor, talk about all that help going to the needy, while they create a new non-productive middle class who have the double advantage of feeding at the public trough and moralizing about the greed of those in business. They snarl at the hand that feeds them. The same is true in the big foundations. They're staffed by closet socialists and egalitarians who think capitalism is a crime and thus dispense the fortunes of robber barons as if they were re-establishing justice. At the same time, they rake in salaries greater than those they could earn in productive work."

"You know a lot about it."

"Mervel, you could not have come to a better man. I had an uncle who was in foundations. So was my aunt." The noise Tuttle made was laughter. Mervel did not join in when the lawyer told him the reference was to women's underwear. Tuttle grew serious. "When I was setting up the Tuttle Foundation I informed myself pretty thoroughly on the subject. There are, as you seem to have surmised, many ways in which these laws can be used against their ostensible purpose. I myself am the director of the Tuttle Foundation. Let us imagine, and it is pure imagination, that there is one million dollars in the endowment of the Tuttle Foundation. There would first of all be the matter of my salary. It could be astronomical, but that would be to bring money within range of the tax collector, and if the original purpose is to avoid tax we have merely postponed it. One could consequently decide to sail close to the wind. Expenses of all sorts might be written off against the foundation. Imagine a crooked Tuttle who would so meld his law practice and the Tuttle Foundation that the many expenses of a law office could in effect be carried by the foundation yet claimed by the law office. And then there is the bookkeeping with respect to grants, bogus grants." Excitement got into the lawyer's voice.

"So you really do have to break the law to take advantage of it?"

"Break the law?" Tuttle seemed to have difficulty with the concept. "No, no. It's not that simple. You must not think that the law is some finished product, covering every contingency. Not at all. Law is negotiated all the time. Take your tax return. Rules and the like are available for many of the things you claim and do not claim. But there is an enormous area wide open to interpretation. If you get called on something, you and/or your lawyer thresh it out with the IRS and some determination is made. Usually a compromise."

"How does that apply to foundations?"

"We would have to know more about your friend in Waukegan." The lawyer darted a shrewd look across his desk. Mervel had hoped Tuttle had forgotten his lucky guess. Fat chance.

"Tuttle, what are the chances the foundation O'Leary is setting up is genuine?"

"About a húndred to one against."

"I'm serious."

"So am I. I watched him on television. A real con artist, if I ever saw one. I checked on the lawyer too. A woman." Tuttle made a face. "And I called a colleague in Waukegan. The rumor is they are sleeping together."

"O'Leary and his lawyer?

"I said she was a woman."

"You know it was O'Leary's wife they found dead in the Stagecoach?"

Tuttle nodded. "Learning about her husband's shenanigans suggested a reason for her suicide. And the visit to Father Dowling."

"What visit to Father Dowling?"

Tuttle looked at him. "That's right, the police kept that to themselves."

"Who told you, Peanuts?"

"I protect my sources as I know you do yours, Mervel."

"Clare O'Leary went to see a priest before committing suicide? I see what you mean."

Mervel was seething at this withholding of information by the police. No wonder, when the priest was Dowling. The pastor of St. Hilary's was an old friend of Keegan's and would be spared any unwanted publicity. But there was a feeling of triumph too, an unlooked-for if dated scoop was in his hands. As Tuttle suggested, it did provide some context for her death. And, when one added the affair between her husband and his lady lawyer, well, things got interesting. The Clare O'Leary Foundation took on added interest as well.

"If you use that Dowling bit, forget where you heard it, okay?"

"How would I use it now? No one is interested in that anymore."

"You seem to be."

"You got me, Counselor. Look, is there any way we could get hold of the details on the foundation?"

"What's your interest?"

"If the guy's a fraud, I want to expose him."

"Why? There are hundreds of frauds right here in town you haven't exposed."

"This guy made an announcement telling us how broken up he is and how generous he is going to be. If he was shacking up with his lawyer, that's already half false. If the rest is false, that is important because he already made it public."

"Thanks to the cooperation of your colleagues."

"Yeah."

They finished the beer. At this time of the day, beer had the effect of water on Mervel but Tuttle had nothing stronger.

Mervel felt completely sober and not a little pleased with himself half an hour later when, having parked his car, he came along the walk to the entrance of his building. He had been ducking his head into the wind and might very easily not have seen Dowling, but he did look up and there across the street was the unmistakable figure of Roger Dowling emerging from the High-Rise. Mervel stopped as if he had run into a plate of Plexiglas. What the hell was Roger Dowling doing in the High-Rise at this hour? It would have been impossible not to think of the Stagecoach Inn and Tuttle's claim that Clare O'Leary had gone to see Dowling. The slender priest with the lean ascetic features gained momentum as he walked away from the hotel and then was gone around a corner. Mervel crossed the street to the High-Rise to see what he could see.

14

WHEN HE returned to his car, Roger Dowling started the motor and waited, holding his watch so that it would catch the light of a lamp in the parking lot. In two minutes he put the car in gear, came onto Hosford, and drew up to the front of the High-Rise. He leaned over to unlock the passenger door. The lobby of the hotel was brightly lighted and empty. He himself had encountered no one when he crossed it from the elevators, and there had been no one behind the desk. The large gaudy room seemed a setting awaiting its action. Roger Dowling yawned. He thought of lighting his pipe, then decided against it. He associated smoking with his study and leisure, not with nervous waiting in the dead of night. Had Zeugner changed his mind? He seemed to think he was safe, staying in the same hotel as those he feared. Only five minutes had passed since they parted. That seemed hard to believe, but the wait of a minute in the parking lot after starting the car had seemed like ten. They should have come down together, but it was the assurance that the car would be waiting at the very door of the hotel with its motor running that had finally persuaded Zeugner he would be far safer in the St. Hilary rectory than in this hotel. Roger Dowling began to think he was more convinced that Zeugner was in danger than was the pianist himself.

Ah, there he was now, loping across the lobby, moving in the lopsided way some dogs have when they run. He should have seemed smaller in that large lobby, but he didn't. Roger Dowling had the impression of a giant of a man, an athlete, coming toward him. The priest slid farther toward the passenger side, so that Zeugner would see it was indeed he awaiting him. That move gave him too good a view of what followed.

Zeugner hesitated before reaching the revolving door and then recognition and relief broke over his face and he came on through the doors. At least he started to. Shooting never sounds like shooting, apparently. Roger Dowling had the impression that someone had started up a pneumatic drill. That made no sense, of course, but the thought came and went. It went when the expression on Zeugner's face changed and his body began to twist and lurch grotesquely. The huge man's knees buckled and then there was the shattering of glass. Roger Dowling instinctively raised an arm, although the window of the car was closed. Blood first appeared running from the corner of Zeugner's mouth. His eyes were locked with the priest's. Whatever momentum he had imparted to the revolving door stopped as he slumped to the floor.

Roger Dowling leaped from his car. He took hold of the revolving door, but he could not move it more than a few inches. "I'm coming," he called out to Zeugner. "I'm coming."

He gave up on the revolving door and entered the hotel by one of the regular doors flanking it. A bewildered unkempt familiar figure cowered in the lobby.

"Help me with the door," Father Dowling cried, and began to tug at the revolving door. But Zeugner's body was too great an obstacle.

Mervel said, "Better leave him be, Father."

This seemed the counsel of despair. Roger Dowling turned to see a woman peering from a doorway behind the registration desk. "Call an ambulance and the police," he called to her. "Do you have first-aid equipment?"

"What's wrong, Father?"

"Where have you been?"

A lie seemed to drift across her mind. "In back."

"This man is seriously wounded."

She had to get on tiptoe to see where Zeugner lay. "Is he a guest?"

She didn't expect an answer, thank God. And then people began to appear, some drifting out from various hiding places, or so it seemed, from behind pillars, moving among the furniture scattered through the lobby. The elevator doors opened all but simultaneously and guests in nightclothes looked out curiously. They seemed to find the sight of a priest both soothing and alarming.

The next ten to fifteen minutes were hectic. A siren's scream was audible moments after the woman clerk had made the phone calls, and then firemen and policemen — she had called both — were busy in the lobby, pushing back the people, giving the ambulance crew the room they needed. Roger Dowling took Mervel aside.

"Did you see what happened?" Roger Dowling asked the reporter.

Mervel nodded and his lips began to tremble. Roger Dowling led him to a couch and they both sat. Mervel looked around. "I was standing by the desk when it happened. Zeugner came out of the elevator and started across the lobby, running, and suddenly this guy pops out of that door and begins blasting away. I just froze. I was sure he would turn the thing on me next. But he stepped back through the door and the next thing I know in you come. Why did you come back?"

"What do you mean?"

"I saw you come out of this hotel and I came in to ask what you'd been doing here."

"I came back for Zeugner." He looked closely at Mervel when he said it, to see if he could surprise there any of the accusing regret he felt himself. If he had let Zeugner stay where he was and where he had wanted to stay.... But clearly the assassin had already discovered he was in the hotel. For the moment Mervel was content to ponder his own all too close encounter with violence.

He nodded at the priest's words but he was not yet ready to re-assume the task of inquisitive newsman that had brought him into mortal danger.

"You'll be able to write an eyewitness report."

Mervel brightened at the idea. A small smile formed on his lips, making him look less weak.

"Would you recognize the gunman again?"

Mervel looked thoughtful, then fearful. His eyes came to the priest's, then flew away. He shook his head.

"It won't matter so far as your story is concerned."

Roger Dowling rose. He had seen Phil Keegan come in. The time was now 1:30. Phil must sleep in his clothes to have gotten here so quickly. The Captain of Detectives was genuinely startled to see Roger Dowling.

"You better give him the last rites, Roger."

"I already did, Phil."

"That's the priest," the woman from behind the desk said. "I told you there was a priest."

"Thanks a lot, lady," Phil said. "Everything's under control now."

"Is he a real priest?" the woman asked.

"We'll find out," Phil assured her. He turned to Roger Dowling. "What happened here?"

"Mervel had a far better view than I did. I was outside. He was inside. He's over here."

Mervel liked the attention but he had been so long on the op-posite side of persistent questioning that he looked as if he might have been willing to forego the honor. Phil Keegan did not visibly react when Mervel explained what had brought him into the hotel.

"And did you find out what Dowling was doing here?"

"I was checking the record."

"You just walked in and began leafing through the record?"

"I identified myself. I offered to look after the desk for a while so she could take a break."

"Very professional."

"Before I got very far, all hell broke loose."

"Tell us about it."

Mervel's version seemed cautious and edited. Either he was saving the details for the story he would write or the lack of them was meant to convey that his knowledge was vague. He seemed anxious to turn the attention of the police on Roger Dowling. Cy Horvath arrived and took Mervel in hand.

"Okay, Roger," Phil said, looking reproachfully at his old friend. "Tell me all about it."

If Roger Dowling noticed that Mervel gave a less than complete account, he knew his own to be, if true, selective. There seemed no way to avoid saying he had returned to the hotel to pick up Zeugner.

"I was going to take him back to the rectory."

"Why?"

"I thought he would be safer there."

"Then he was expecting what happened?"

Could anyone have expected what had happened? Zeugner had been afraid, but it was almost a calm fear. He had interpreted what had been said to him by Maxwell in a certain way and he was prepared to act on it. His interpretation seemed justified now. Still, Roger Dowling could not say Zeugner had expected to be shot down as he had been.

"Who was he afraid of?"

"It had to do with the place he worked. The Stagecoach Inn. He felt that the things that had been happening there put him in a bad light."

"Had he been threatened?"

"He felt in danger."

Keegan shook his head. "And you thought he should be transferred to your maximum-security parish house? Come on, Roger."

"What exactly did the person who called you about Zeugner say?"

Phil thought. "I don't know the exact words. Something about Zeugner and Mrs. O'Leary."

"Ah."

"Did Zeugner talk about Mrs. O'Leary?"

"He knew her, of course."

"Why of course?"

"She spoke to him in the bar where he played piano."

On the verge of telling Phil all he knew, Roger Dowling was interrupted by a more pressing obligation. The paramedics called to him.

"Better come, Father."

The priest hurried to Zeugner and accompanied him to the ambulance, praying as the paramedics worked desperately on the big man.

He did not go back inside after the ambulance drove away. His own car still stood at the curb. He looked back into the lobby, but Phil was caught up in activity. Roger Dowling got into his car and drove home through the deserted streets of Fox River.

He put the car in the garage and the door, when he lowered it, sounded as if it would announce the end of the world. Nor was he particularly quiet getting into the house. As he passed the study, he heard the buzzer on his phone. He went in and picked it up.

"Yes, Marie. Everything is fine."

"I thought that was you but I wanted to make sure."

"Good night, Marie."

He settled behind the desk and picked up a pipe and began to fill it slowly. Out of the whole mad turmoil of the evening one fact came forward, as if it made the rest intelligible. Clare O'Leary had been to the Stagecoach before. She had not chosen it randomly on the day she died. Twinkie Zeugner had known her for several weeks, maybe even for months.

15

PHIL KEEGAN had been in bed when the call came about the shooting in the High-Rise Hotel but not really asleep. He got back home again after five and slept fitfully until he got up once more at seven. It was not yet eight o'clock when he sat down at the table in the St. Hilary rectory dining room and Marie Murkin put a cup of hot coffee before him. Now that he was up he felt sleepy and he wondered if even three or four cups of Mrs. Murkin's coffee would get him through this day.

"You're out early," Marie said, lingering in the dining room.

"And your boss was out late."

"I'm asleep with the birds. Were the two of you up to something?"

"Would you tell him I'm here? He's expecting me."

"I let him know when I saw you drive up."

"Have you listened to the news this morning?"

"I could turn it on."

"Thanks. Do you get the *Messenger* here?"

Marie pulled out a chair and sat. "What's this all about? I've never seen you like this before."

"Things on my mind."

"I know what you mean." Marie Murkin sighed.

It pained Keegan to think that the days of his friendship with Roger Dowling were over and that he might never again sit at this table. Memories of beer and popcorn and Cub games teased his mind, but he drove them away. Roger was making a fool of him, preventing him from performing his job. What kind of a friend is that? But he had not come for an apology or to find out what specious reasons Roger might have had. All he wanted was a no-nonsense, full-out account of what Roger Dowling had been doing at the High-Rise. The priest was the witness of a murder and that is the way Phil Keegan intended to treat him. That is why, when the pastor of St. Hilary's entered, the Captain of Detectives of the Fox River Police Department rose from his chair.

"Good morning, Father Dowling."

"The same to you, Captain Keegan."

Marie Murkin looked at the two men and skittered into her kitchen. There was the sound of the radio being turned on.

"Sit down, Phil."

Keegan managed to do so in perfect synchrony with Roger Dowling.

"Zeugner is dead. I want to know everything he told you when you went down to talk with him. First of all, why didn't he come here?"

"He was afraid the rectory was being watched by the police."

"You're kidding."

"No. During the phone conversation, I mentioned that the police had received a call suggesting they look into his relations with Clare O'Leary. He assumed he would be arrested as soon as he was recognized."

"Is that why he was at the High-Rise?"

"No. He was already there when he learned about the call."

"So why was he there?"

"His boss had suggested to him a few hours earlier that he take early retirement. Go live in Florida. He interpreted that as a threat."

"Why?"

"He said he knew too much to be allowed to retire."

"He said that?"

"Yes. He mentioned the drug traffic at the Stagecoach Inn."

But that wasn't the worst of it. Zeugner himself was an addict. He took mainly cocaine and marijuana, which he insisted were not addictive, but at the same time his only concern about his future was his drug supply."

"The autopsy showed he was full of the stuff. So he meant his boss was going to rub him out."

"He even felt he had met his assassin."

"Did he say who he worked for?"

"A man named Maxwell. He had worked for him since he was quite a young man. He felt that Maxwell blamed him for the O'Leary woman's death."

"Why?"

"Phil, Clare O'Leary had been at the Stagecoach Inn before. Zeugner knew her."

Keegan shook his head. "Why the hell didn't you talk like this last night instead of trying to speak without saying anything? Now here you are this morning telling me everything I have to know."

"You're right to be annoyed, Phil. I was more shaken up last night than I realized. Think of it. I had seen a man killed right before my eyes, a man I had just been talking to and who was coming to get into my car when he was shot. Shot! How many bullets struck the man, Phil?"

"At least eleven. Well, it cured his habit. You did give him the Last Sacraments?"

Roger Dowling nodded. Keegan felt no inclination to go into deep mourning because a nightclub entertainer, cocaine sniffer, and smoker of pot should have been hurtled into heaven after being cut down by a dozen bullets.

"Did Maxwell telephone Zeugner or what?"

"They talked in the High-Rise. Maxwell was staying there."

Keegan just stared at the priest, then pushed back from the table and went down the hall to the study. He got through to the High-Rise and to Cy Horvath. He waited while Cy checked.

"Zeugner wasn't registered either, Captain. As far as the records go, he just happened to be in the hotel early this morning."

"Thanks, Cy."

Keegan went back to the dining room and gave Dowling the news. The priest frowned.

"Well, Zeugner was registered under another name. O'Toole, I think. Whoever registered him should remember. He had no luggage and said something about an airline, as if it had been lost and would be sent to the hotel. Maybe Maxwell used another name too."

"He told you he talked to Maxwell in that hotel, was scared to death, and then holed up there himself?"

"He regarded that as very shrewd. When he left Maxwell's room he felt he was being followed, so he got off the elevator at the mezzanine, verified that someone was following him, waited until the man returned to Maxwell, then registered himself as Mr. O'Toole."

"Maxwell will probably be able to prove that he was in Florida at the time."

There was a small scream from the kitchen and then the door flew open and Marie Murkin stood there, ashen-faced, staring at Father Dowling.

"He was killed last night! The man who phoned you was murdered."

"Everything's under control," Keegan assured her. He hated it when women lost control. You couldn't just shake them the way you could men.

Not that Phil Keegan blamed Marie Murkin for being upset by what Dowling had done. It was one thing for a dying man to get the Last Sacraments, but Keegan saw no justification at all for the priest's answering a summons in the middle of the night that put not only himself but the man he was going to see in danger.

"I was never in any danger, Phil."

"No? Well, you are now."

"In what way?"

"Maxwell, or whoever killed Zeugner, now knows you were the last one to talk with him. They will assume he told everything he knew to a priest. Whatever he knew that they regarded as threatening, you now know."

"And so do you, Phil. I've told you everything Zeugner told me."

He had no immediate answer to that, but he was sure there was one. It was Marie Murkin he promised that St. Hilary's rectory would be under police protection for the indefinite future. He felt reconciled with Roger Dowling because of the priest's willingness to tell him everything he knew that could help in finding Zeugner's murderer. But he still felt much of the pique that had brought him here this morning and he liked the faintly punitive as well as protective aspect of his promise. It wasn't the first time Dowling had wandered into danger and it did not help to be told he was simply doing his job as a priest when this happened. Keegan certainly did not think someone should call up a rectory at whatever time of the day or night, even a man like Twinkie Zeugner, and be told to go peddle his papers. But Roger Dowling should have called his old friend Phil Keegan before going down to the High-Rise. That could have been on an unofficial basis and certainly it would not have jeopardized Zeugner. He was under no danger of arrest because of the anonymous phone call that had come into police headquarters. The poor son of a bitch. What a way to go after the life he had led. Keegan did not think of playing the piano in a nightclub as work, and the fact that Zeugner had been on drugs added to the notion of a social parasite, a drone. The guy could have been a professional athlete, thereby engaging in what Keegan regarded as socially worthwhile activity. And then that name. Twinkie. Good God. Still, they said he had wowed the ladies at the Stagecoach Inn, among them Clare O'Leary.

"Whether or not there was anything else, the two of them were friends, Clare O'Leary and Zeugner?"

Dowling nodded. "And now both are dead."

"You think there's a connection?"

"Surely you do."

"Nothing is sure until it's sure, Roger. She committed suicide and he was gunned down mob style. So they knew each other. Was she on the stuff too?"

"Drugs? I don't know, Phil. Zeugner didn't say. You have to remember that I was looking forward to getting him back here so we could have a real talk. He was ashamed to talk about her, for whatever significance that might have."

"But you got no inkling why she went to the Stagecoach?"

"I didn't get the impression that it was to see Zeugner, but that might have been the result of his sheepishness in talking about her. He seemed to expect me to start scolding him."

"Well, there is one obvious reason for her going there, given the trafficking that takes place in the motel. I have asked Phelps to do another autopsy. He is in the process of making a decision. Robertson is neutral. The one autopsy I have says the only substance found in her body was sleeping pills."

"Something like that should be settled one way or another. If she didn't go there to see Zeugner, and if drugs weren't her motivation, what was her reason?"

"We can always go back to what she told you."

"Yes. And that would turn your attention to Larry O'Leary."

"God forbid. Did you read in the paper about his plans for his money?"

"I got it from a more direct source. The Reverend David Hogan. Hogan makes me skeptical of legends about the saints. He seems prepared to canonize O'Leary. I wish I could see what the man is doing as something more than a gesture."

"He's welcome to his lawyer, if that's the next step."

"If it is, you had better take Clare O'Leary's story more seriously."

"Roger, I have excluded nothing, believe me. Absolutely nothing."

For what that was worth. It came down to the admission that they did not know where the hell they were. That is why he headed back downtown. Sticking around for Dowling's noon Mass was out of the question today. There was no way he could avoid reporting to Robertson on what had happened last night at the High-Rise. First he wanted to swing by the hotel and see if Cy had come up with anything new.

Agnes Lamb was talking to the clerk Mervel had bribed in order to get a look at the registration and Cy was with the one who had had duty the day before. Both subjects had expressions suggesting they were somewhere between tears and uncontrolled rage at the treatment they were getting. Perhaps their word had never been so systematically questioned before. Keegan pulled a chair up next to Agnes Lamb's. The black officer took no notice of him. She sighed eloquently, then said in bored tones to the chubby, bleached, and now probably racist clerk who was having trouble lighting her cigarette with a plastic throwaway lighter, "If you were behind the desk when Mervel came in, you must have seen the gunman. Mervel says he was not at the desk a full minute before the shooting began. You took Mervel's money and came back here. The shooting started. You, my dear, claim not to have heard it! It wakened the manager, it brought guests on the run and people in from the street even at that hour of the night, and you say you didn't hear it?"

"If I did I didn't think it was what it was."

"Are you hard of hearing, Bridget?"

"No!"

"Is there deafness in your family — father, mother?"

"We all have perfect hearing in my family," Bridget said icily. She was trying to return her unlit cigarette to its package.

"Can you imagine what a hostile lawyer would do with that remark? Let me tell you something else that will occur to a hostile lawyer. He is going to think you set Zeugner up. He came out of the elevator and almost immediately is shot. Was that the signal, your coming back here?"

"I came back here because that reporter..."

Keegan slipped away. Lamb was good. He found it easier to

accept this now. He told himself it was because she was a woman — being black had nothing to do with it — that he had been sure she would never make a cop. Horvath had told him he was wrong and now Keegan knew he had been.

The clerk Cy was interviewing was a real twinkletoes. He made a wet noise with his mouth before speaking and rolled his eyes in resignation when Cy kept at him relentlessly.

"Let's start over again and consolidate what we've learned, Dale. You remember registering Mr. Zeugner."

"I remember registering Mr. O'Toole, whom you say is Mr. Zeugner."

"We'll verify that at the morgue."

Dale's eyes rounded. "I refuse to look at a dead body."

Cy ignored that. "Very well. O'Toole/Zeugner had entered the hotel an hour or so before he registered in order to visit Mr. Maxwell. Did you register Mr. Maxwell?"

"We checked the record and there is — and was — no Maxwell registered."

"That's right. Just as there was no Zeugner registered. Things do get odd on your shift, don't they, Dale? Now, by elimination, we have concluded that Maxwell was occupying the bridal suite on the fourteenth floor."

"Presidential suite. A Mr. Neenan was registered there."

"Yes. Since the day before yesterday. What can you tell us of Mr. Neenan?"

"Nothing. I don't remember a thing about him."

"Yet you registered him. Surely it's not every day that you put someone in the bridal suite. That should have stuck in your mind. The question becomes, why hasn't it? There is one possible explanation that occurs to me. You have a reason for not remembering. That reason might be money, it might be fear, it might be any number of things. We can explore them all, Dale. We are going to get to the bottom of this."

Well, Keegan thought, if we do, it won't be through these clerks. He was all for such routine questioning, don't get him

□ 98 □

wrong; he was its great champion. Small items, no one of them important in itself, accumulated to point a direction or suggest a way to the significant fact. It took patience, and Cy and Agnes were patient. They did not expect miracles and that was important.

Dale asked permission to go to the lavatory and for a moment it seemed that Cy would deny it. After he agreed, reluctantly, Keegan was able to ask him if there was anything new.

"Zeugner's room was visible from the parking lot below. Presuming the room has been left untouched, the drape was open about three feet. It's possible someone saw Zeugner or maybe Dowling and that's the explanation. These clerks don't know anything."

"Why don't you and Agnes switch subjects?"

"We did, about fifteen minutes before you came."

"I'm going down to talk with Robertson."

"Lots of luck."

16

TUTTLE was impressed and he wasn't reluctant to say so.

"You're a cool bastard, Mervel. I'll give you that. You leave my place, drop by the High-Rise and witness a gang killing, tap it out for the *Messenger*, and then come up here to sleep the sleep of the just."

Mervel had assured Tuttle that the lawyer was one of the few who knew the location of the reporter's quarters. That was Tuttle's phrase for the apartment: The Reporter's Quarters. If Mervel liked it he gave no indication. The apartment was an ungodly mess but nonetheless attractive. Excessive drinking seemed to go with the place and Tuttle was not really surprised when at eleven in the morning Mervel offered him a whisky.

"The story is being picked up by the wire services too, Tuttle. Fame, wealth, job offers from the real world." Mervel seemed unexcited by any aspect of this.

"Tell me about it," Tuttle said, putting down his barely sipped drink.

"I thought you read my story."

"I want the unexpurgated version, Mervel. The blood and the gore. I would have been scared out of my boots."

"It was over before I knew what was happening, Tuttle. It has given me a new understanding of courage." Mervel drank thoughtfully. He remained silent for a moment after taking his glass from his lips. "Courage is ignorance in action."

Tuttle ducked into his drink so he wouldn't have to comment on that. Tuttle was less impressed than he had been on the way over here.

"You taking the day off?"

"Tuttle, I didn't get home until after five in the morning. And you call at nine-thirty."

"As soon as I saw the paper. I don't always read the *Messenger*."

Mervel did not take offense. The truth was that the Fox River *Messenger* should have died a dignified death years before, but the family that owned it refused to believe people considered themselves citizens of Chicago, not Fox River, and preferred the *Trib* or the *Sun-Times* to the *Messenger*. Maybe the days of the Chicago dailies are numbered too. Tuttle and Mervel had had this conversation before.

"I know, I know, I booked passage on the Titanic when I entered journalism. I suppose Bruce Wiggins has a crew at the High-Rise so he can broadcast an eyewitness account of what happened." Mervel could not keep the venom from his voice when he mentioned Wiggins. In Tuttle's opinion, Mervel should make the move to television while he still had a chance, even if it meant writing scripts for pretty boys like Wiggins.

"Whatever you write now is read by someone else, isn't it? So have it read by an expert."

"It would be read by Wiggins."

So Mervel was beyond the reach of reason. But rancor stirred Mervel into complete wakefulness and he went into the bathroom to shower and shave. It seemed a good time for Tuttle to catch up on some phone calls.

The police operator was reluctant to put Peanuts on even — or was it when — Tuttle identified himself as senior partner in Tuttle and Tuttle and a good friend of officer Pianone. Perhaps she thought he was a smart defense lawyer trying to con a cop into telling him things he shouldn't know. A nostalgic smile distorted Tuttle's lips at this imagined accusation. If he were further from the Poor Farm than he was he would have been capable of enjoying the memories of the early days of his firm. What little success he had had was due in large part to his friendship with Peanuts Pianone. In another place and time, the Pianones might have solved the problem of Peanuts by entering him in a religious order. As it was, they put him into the Fox River police force, something which, with two members of the family on the city council, they were able to do despite Peanuts' difficulty with the tests. Some candidates flunked the test. Peanuts had been unable even to take it. This and other requirements were waived and the chubby little man with the strange hairline and eyes narrow with animal wariness became a cop.

Was the family thereby in the enemy camp or vice versa? There were Pianones who had their doubts, but Peanuts ended by placating everyone on the force. He was so dumb he was impossible to hate. Tuttle found Peanuts likable. Indeed, in moments of reflection, when the lawyer asked himself who his closest friend was, he had difficulty not thinking of Peanuts. So he stopped thinking. There was something devastating in the thought that the closest he had come to human closeness was Peanuts Pianone. He preferred to think that he shrewdly used Peanuts for his own purposes.

Eventually he persuaded the operator to put him through to Peanuts. Peanuts picked up his phone on the first ring. Tuttle identified himself and asked Peanuts what case he was working on.

"Harley."

Tuttle had to think. *Sic transit*, or whatever the saying was. It sounded like an indisposed trolley. Harley had been a force in his day and had ended up hanging in a shower in the Sleepytime Motel. Tuttle shuddered with what he hoped was not a premonition of his own end. "How's it look?"

"That's hard to say."

"They got you on it all alone?"

"That's all right with me. I don't want that goddamn Agnes Lamb with me."

Peanuts was a racist. His whole family was racist. It was not independently that Pianone had come to convictions about his own genetic superiority.

"I can't tell you, Tuttle."

"Do you know?"

"Yeah, but I can't tell you."

As he had on other occasions, Tuttle felt the clammy grip of fear. If Peanuts ever did tell him something the Pianones preferred he did not know, Tuttle might end up hanging in a motel shower himself. Dear God, was that the explanation of Harley?

He said, "They're still talking about Clare O'Leary?"

"Yeah."

"What do you think of the guy who got it at the High-Rise last night?"

"Whatcha want, Tuttle?" Peanuts asked.

"Just called to say hello, Peanuts. It's been a while. I think I'll run up to Waukegan this afternoon on business."

"Keep it at fifty-five."

The weird sound on the phone was Peanuts laughing. Tuttle held the instrument away from him and stared at it before returning it to its cradle. Peanuts laughing was like a rhesus monkey playing chess.

17

WILMA didn't want to see anybody and she didn't want to talk to anybody. All she wanted to do is what she was doing, hiding out in the physical fitness center, door locked, working out in a totally mindless way. The parallel bars, the rings, weights, and then she sat in the sauna until she was sure she would cook. It worked for a time, for a long time, but finally she had to think about poor Twinkie.

Kaye, one of the waitresses in the Billet-Doux, had told her. She might have been mentioning a weather report or just some item you read of in the paper — farmer killed by overturned tractor, child asphyxiated, worker falls. All dreadful happenings maybe, but if you didn't know the people involved what could you feel that made any sense? But Kaye had been speaking of Twinkie, the man whose singing she had been hearing non-stop for months during her working hours.

Wilma just stared at Kaye, horrified, and then she turned and ran to the elevators. She got into one but its doors would not close, they were timed for definite intervals; she kept punching the Close button anyway, and finally the doors did close and she was rising swiftly up the shaft to her physical fitness room. She managed not to cry until she was safely inside and had the door locked.

At first she simply moaned; the sound frightened her, although it was a great relief to fill the physical fitness center with that toneless wail of grief. It seemed to her now that she and Twinkie actually had been far closer than they had been, that he preferred being with her to anything, and that eventually, well, something permanent would have emerged. He had had a massive indifference to women; so far as Wilma knew there was no woman in his life, but that could be explained by the Billet-Doux. A man might think he wanted all that attention, but it was pretty obvious it was a pain in the neck. Twinkie had liked to come up here where the two of them could be alone and just talk, ordinary talk, normal talk, not more of that goddamned joshing he had to engage in with the customers.

Someone began to rattle the locked door. Wilma stopped howling and took several very deep breaths, getting herself under control. She didn't intend to open the door, but she was afraid someone had heard her moan. The doors kept on rattling and someone called her name. It was Kaye.

"I'm not open," Wilma called through the door.

"Let me in. Please!" More rattling. It seemed clear Kaye would stand out there rattling the door until it was opened.

Wilma unlocked the door and pulled it open. Kaye just stood there, an abject expression on her face. There were tears in her eyes. And then she came and took Wilma in her arms and the two of them stood there sobbing. It was the dumbest thing you ever saw. Wilma thought so even at the time, but it was such a relief to be able to cry like that and have someone sympathetic help you through it.

"I just wasn't thinking," Kaye said, shaking her head. She closed the door and turned the key. "You got coffee here or anything?"

"I'll make some."

Wasn't that the myth? The grieving woman busies herself with household chores. Wilma's instinct had been to exercise, but maybe it came to the same thing. Kaye got clumsily onto a horse and sat there sidesaddle.

"You hadn't heard, had you, Wilma?"

She shook her head. It seemed best not to try to use her voice just yet.

"And I had to be the one to tell you."

Kaye lit up a cigarette when the coffee was ready and smoked steadily from then on, but Wilma did not object. That smoking or lack of exercise or a bad diet might affect one's health and thus one's life expectancy suddenly seemed a silly concern. Twinkie was dead and she was alive but it wasn't because she kept herself in good condition and he had not. Kaye babbled on and Wilma learned more than she would have thought she wanted to know. How did Kaye know so many details?

"Guess who's a maintenance man at the High-Rise? My Carl. He had a grandstand seat all morning while police were all over the place."

Carl had heard it all, where the first bullet had struck Twinkie and then the whole barrage as he tried to spin through the revolving door. And that is where he died, stuck in the revolving door.

"But a priest got to him, pushed right in there and blessed him or whatever."

"Oh, good!"

"You a Catholic, Wilma?"

"No, but Twinkie was. Used to be. I guess they never really leave. He was raised Catholic and I think he still held to it. Anyway, I'm glad."

"Does that mean he goes to heaven, is that what they believe?"

"Something like that. I'm not sure. How come a priest was there at that time of night?"

"Search me. Funny. It was the same one Mrs. O'Leary went to see the day she died. He sounds to me like someone to stay away from."

"What's his name?"

"I forget. It's in the paper, though. Wilma, I know how you felt about Twinkie, but was he fooling around with the O'Leary woman?"

"No!" She relaxed. "I don't know. I don't think so."

"Maybe it's that priest, but I'm wondering if the two are connected. She dies, Twinkie dies. Do you know the one I'm thinking of?"

"No."

"The guy Mrs. O'Leary met here."

Wilma looked blankly at Kaye. The waitress wore her dyed hair piled high on her head and her skirt was too short, binding her hips.

"Geez, you really are on Cloud Nine up here, aren't you? Don't you know anything that's going on around here? The O'Leary woman came here to see some guy. They checked in separately but they were here together. It must be nice when you can afford two rooms when you only need one."

"Who told you all this?"

"Honey, when you see them in the dark of the Billet-Doux you know what's going on. I suggested he could charge what they ordered to their room, and she laughed. He told me they were in different rooms. I couldn't believe it. So I checked with Hilda and got the story. Let me tell you, it was a relief. If I start reading people wrong in that department I am not going to be much of a waitress."

Wilma had the impression Kaye was talking about the moon when she talked about the Stagecoach; it was at least as strange a place as the cocktail waitress chattered on about it. The little mound of filters saturated with harmful juices seemed more noxious than the smoke of one of Kaye's freshly lit cigarettes. Didn't she realize there was that much gunk and more in her lungs? Wilma felt her old self coming back. Kaye's story suggested something she might do, a sort of memorial for Twinkie. If Mrs. O'Leary had met someone at the Stagecoach and if that someone thought Twinkie Zeugner was his rival with Mrs. O'Leary, there was a motive to kill Twinkie that could be shared by her husband and her lover. Why suicide? Wilma could imagine a woman caught in an impossible situation, between two men, maybe three, ye gods, her only out a bottle of pills. But Twinkie had been murdered.

"The police must know about that man, Kaye."

"I don't think they learned much around here, do you? No one wanted to talk to that black cop, not even the maids. Affirmative action, wow."

"But they should be told."

"Yeah? Well, not by me. Look at what happened to Twinkie."

"What do you mean?"

Kaye mashed a half-smoked cigarette in the ashtray. "Not a thing. I'm sticking to my original theory. Mrs. O'Leary's lover boy."

"I wonder who he was."

"I thought of taking a peek at the registration cards, but I doubt that would help. If you were keeping a rendezvous in a motel you wouldn't register in your own name."

"Why not? Mrs. O'Leary did."

"I meant men. Men are sneakier than women."

That got her going on Carl. Wilma didn't offer her a second cup of coffee, but Kaye got off the horse and made one for herself. Wilma didn't really mind. She knew she was going to do something, but she didn't know what it was. In the meantime, Kaye's ceaseless talking formed a soothing background against which to think. Or, if not to think, to wait for some inspiration to come out of the void.

And it did come, like something predestined. It was perfectly obvious, once she thought of it. She would go see that priest, whatever his name was. She would look it up in the paper and then go see him. She would ask him if he knew of the man Clare O'Leary had come to the Stagecoach to see.

18

PHIL KEEGAN'S request for a re-examination of Clare O'Leary's body, surprisingly okayed by Robertson, brought Larry O'Leary, his lawyer, and his pastor bustling down to Fox River, and eventually this entailed another visit by the Reverend David Hogan to the St. Hilary rectory.

"Doesn't a person's good name mean anything anymore, Roger? Do you have any cigarettes here?"

"How about a cigar?" Hogan accepted one and prepared to light it. "I don't see how this can harm Larry O'Leary's reputation."

"I was thinking of hers, Roger. Clare's."

"If there were a reversal of the judgment of suicide?"

Hogan shrugged. "I don't like it. Frankly, the police in this town seem a capricious lot. Not at all professional."

Roger Dowling felt resentment rise in him and he realized that he was offended by the implied criticism of Phil Keegan and his department. "I suppose it's always harder when the culprits come in from elsewhere."

"I asked Larry and Andrea Kruger to meet me here when they're through with the police. I hope that's all right?"

"Of course," Roger Dowling said dubiously. The prospect of seeing again the unctuous Larry O'Leary was less than joyous. "Meantime, you and I can go over to the parish center."

Hogan raised the hand that held the cigar. "Please, Roger. No guided tours. I promise to spare you when you visit me."

"This isn't a tour. We've turned our school into a center where elderly people spend a good portion of their day. You might want to talk with Edna Hospers. It could give you ideas for your parish."

"Roger, the average adult in my parish is less than forty."

"Well, time flies. Before you know it they'll be demanding something like our center. Do you have a school?"

"Haven't you heard, Roger? Parish schools are too big an expense to be taken on lightly. Our kids are bused."

"Tell me about it while we walk over to the center."

This seemed compromise enough to Hogan. When they were on their way to the school Roger Dowling saw a young woman come out the side door of the church and look around in confusion.

"Wait a minute, Dave," he said, and detoured down the walk to the church. The woman came toward him, her gait somewhat mannish.

"Hello," Father Dowling said. "Can I help you?"

"Are you Father Dowling?"

"That's right."

"I came to see you." Her eyes went past him to Father Hogan. Roger Dowling tried not to feel too delighted that pastoral duty now forced him to send Dave Hogan on to the parish center alone.

Five minutes later, having put Dave Hogan in the capable hands of Edna Hospers, Roger Dowling sat in the front parlor with the young woman who had identified herself as Wilma Goudge.

"We pronounce it Goodge but it's spelled G-o-u-d-g-e. I've always hated it, almost as much as my given name."

"I had an Aunt Wilma." That was stretching it a bit. He had had a friend whose aunt was named Wilma, but he had always considered her his own as well. "They actually called her Will."

The woman laughed but she was clearly nervous. "I've never talked with a priest before. I expected to find you in the church."

"I'm not there all the time," he said. In B movies priests were always in their churches, lurking behind a pillar, trimming candles, sometimes praying.

"I work at the Stagecoach Inn. I'm in charge of the physical fitness center." Her chin tilted and she looked him straight in the eye as if she thought he might disapprove of her work.

"That has been the scene of a great deal of excitement lately, hasn't it? A suicide and then the Twinkie Zeugner killing."

"You were with him when he died, weren't you?"

"Yes, I was."

"He would have liked that. We were good friends, Twinkie and me."

The reason Wilma Goudge had come to see him was that she remembered he had been visited by Mrs. O'Leary before she died. He said that made him sound like a dangerous person to consult, but she was not to be deflected from her aim now that she was actually sitting here talking to a priest. Not that it was easy for Roger Dowling to figure out her aim. She seemed to be proceeding under the assumption that two things related to each other were related to a third thing.

"You mean someone who killed them both?"

"Someone who killed Twinkie, anyway. And why? Some people thought there was something going on there, between Twinkie and Mrs. O'Leary."

"Was there?"

"I don't know. But if someone thought there was, that's just as bad."

"You're not inventing this third party, are you?"

"I just found out there was someone Mrs. O'Leary met at the Stagecoach."

"Who told you?"

"I seem to be the only one who doesn't know."

"The police don't know."

"Oh, no one would tell them."

"Why? Don't they want Twinkie's killer found?"

"I do. That's why I'm here. I thought if I told you and you passed it on, then nobody could tell how the police found out."

"Who is everyone afraid of?"

She ignored the question. "They can check the register but he may not have used his own name."

"What does he look like?"

"I'm no good at describing people."

She must know that once the police got going on this they would turn the Stagecoach Inn upside down until they found out who the man was. He assured her he would see that the police were told.

"Why did she come see you the day she died?"

"It isn't confidential. She didn't tell me anything others don't know. She had left her husband. She feared for her life. I suppose she hoped I'd endorse her decision."

After Wilma Goudge left and he had gone into the study for a pipe, he wondered if he did know why Clare had come to him. It seemed inescapable that she had deliberately misled him. She had not said in so many words that this was her first visit to Fox River, but that was a fair inference from what she had told him. She had fled her husband who threatened to kill her. That had been the nub of it. Her apparent reason for coming to him was that she sought the counsel of a priest. He had accepted the image as a threatened and discarded wife. The emerging truth was light-years different. It appeared that she was the unfaithful party and she had sat here talking with him while intending later that day to meet a man. And then commit suicide? Roger Dowling found it easier to imagine the infidelity — flesh is weak, and not just feminine flesh — but he would never be able to believe that the woman he had talked with intended to commit suicide or, indeed, could have brought herself to do it.

The phone rang and he picked it up. It was Edna Hospers.

"Father Hogan wondered if you'd be much longer."

Good Lord, he had forgotten all about his visitor from Waukegan. "I'll be right over."

"He says the same thing."

So they met on the sidewalk. Roger Dowling was still wondering if it would worsen matters if he apologized. Hogan wore a sour and preoccupied look. A car pulled up at the curb, a horn sounded, and out bounded Larry O'Leary. He came across the lawn toward them with Andrea Kohler hurrying along after him.

"We are going to sue this whole damned city and everyone in it. Not you, Father Dowling. Do you know what they claim their second autopsy showed? Traces of drugs other than sleeping pills. I wonder what the third autopsy will indicate? Leprosy? Father, do you have a drink?"

"Good idea," Hogan chimed in, and the two hurried toward the rectory.

Father Dowling turned to Andrea Kohler. "Did you know Clare took drugs?"

"No, but maybe we shouldn't be surprised. It explains a good deal of her odd behavior. And excuses it, at least up to a point. I know I feel less angered by what she said about me." She took a deep breath. "Look, if you want to go in with the others, go ahead. I am going to stroll around and enjoy this weather."

"Mrs. Murkin will take care of them. Come. I'll show you my garden."

Not even Phil Keegan was impressed by what he called his garden and Mrs. Murkin found it derisory. Roger Dowling had a city boy's ignorance of and fascination with the soil and it had entered his head that he could, in the famous phrase, having left the world behind, literally cultivate his garden. Not all the seeds he bought proved worth the price. Some germinated but did not survive. He had had good luck with irises, however. It was like a Gospel parable. Andrea Kohler was preoccupied and unlikely to condemn or praise his horticultural efforts.

He said, "Drugs could explain another surprising bit of Clare's conduct. There seems reason to believe that not only had she come to the Stagecoach Inn several times before, but on the last occasion she met a man. By prearrangement."

"A rendezvous?" She seemed delighted.

"That's what I'm told."

"Who is he?"

"He hasn't been identified yet."

"That is someone I would very much like to meet. Clare! What a surprising little vixen she was. Imagine making up those stories about Larry and me and then meeting a man in a Fox River motel."

He did not tell her that this man would immediately become a suspect in the death of Twinkie Zeugner. He did not want to tell Andrea Kohler about the suggested liaison between Clare and Twinkie Zeugner. It would have seemed disloyal to provide the woman Clare had professed to see as her rival with gossip like that.

"I think I *would* like a drink, Father."

Her step was quick as they went to the house. It seemed obvious that she couldn't wait to tell Larry O'Leary what she had learned. But she kept it to herself there in the rectory. Perhaps she wanted to get him away from Father Hogan before she told him. For his part, Roger Dowling wanted to talk to Phil Keegan about Wilma Goudge's visit, and he was grateful Andrea Kohler got the three of them on the move back to Waukegan.

19

THERE was no way she was going to tell Larry what she had learned from Father Dowling while Dave Hogan was with them and, driving back to Waukegan — it was like the two of them to accept unhesitatingly when she offered to drive — she tuned out the superficial male chatter and welcomed the monotony of the road. Larry sat beside her, turned sideways, his arm over the back of the seat, the better to carry on his conversation with Hogan. They were comparing Hogan's parish with Roger Dowling's, to the detriment of the latter. Honest to God, you'd think Larry was a priest himself. He loved clerical gossip. Andrea, not for the first time, felt a twinge of sympathy with Clare.

Clare! What a most surprising little wench she had been. Andrea's first impression had been of a woman it would be ridiculously easy to deceive. But her first suspicions had been of Larry. He came on, in the phrase — how phrases date one — like gangbusters, and Andrea had waited for the pitch. Waited with the intention of really letting him have it, the goddamn male chauvinist. How often she rehearsed the little scene in which she would flatten him, destroy him. After he made his move. But he had not made a move. Andrea was puzzled, then annoyed, and, in the end, she began to lead him on, still intent on crushing him when he responded. After all, no matter how he propositioned her — even if it were after a little enticement, not to say entrapment — doing so would be guilt enough and she would tell him what she thought of him. On behalf of the women of the world.

That somewhat ironic estimate came later, much later, but it had been implicit in her actions from the beginning. Why, when you thought of it, she was leading Larry on as a favor to Clare, to show her that he was like the rest of men. But any thought that she was wronging Clare was already alleviated by the almost textbook character of Clare's acceptance of her secondary status. Whatever Larry wanted, she wanted; what Larry decided was quite simply the last word. His outrageously tasteless way of referring to her on the radio provided Andrea with her wedge. Larry might think he was joking when he referred to his wife as a drag on his life, a negative force, a burden, and all the rest — the wife as comic foil — but Andrea became convinced that two things were going on. First, and obviously, the jokes were a way of reinforcing Clare's already low estimate of herself, and second, Larry really and truly, if subconsciously, wanted to get rid of his wife. Andrea was surprised that others did not see this. But of course they didn't, Clare least of all. That is when Andrea decided to bring matters into the open by getting Clare to see those jokes as real threats to her life.

Perhaps Andrea would have lost interest in all that if Larry had not suddenly, without warning, succumbed to her come-hither efforts.

Clare had been visiting an old girl friend in Florida at the time and Larry, in a way she was coming to see as typical, wanted to tinker with the provisions of his will. There was a side of him that regarded such success as he had gained as a divine judgment. The rich man and the needle's eye, that sort of thing. By making and remaking his will, disposing of and thus distancing himself from his worldly goods, he was trying to stave off damnation. She had come to his house, which was silly. You would have thought there was an emergency involved in the fact that he had just learned of an obscure community of contemplative nuns to which he wished to leave ten thousand dollars. His will already read like a list of Catholic charities.

Perhaps it was to prevent herself from showing her impatience that Andrea had two very strong drinks. Of course she was already miffed with him for other reasons. He was not doing much for her own self-esteem by simply ignoring her all but open invitations. That she was older than Larry simply did not enter into her way of viewing the situation. Since making the big break from Jack and the kids, Andrea had felt her life literally beginning again. On that estimate, she was in her late twenties. There was no reason at all why they couldn't, in a phrase that didn't date her, make it.

So if the original idea was that, when Larry finally made his move, she would lower the boom on him, it didn't work out that way. They were in Larry's study, a very nice, very masculine room: leather chairs, lots of brass and darkish furniture, well polished, and heavy drapes in a shade of green that had always enthralled Andrea. Isn't our search for the right clothes in large part a search for the exact shade of a particular color that is ours in a predestined way? Andrea thought so and there was her color hanging on the windows of Larry O'Leary's study. Work done, the contemplative nuns provided for, Andrea put away her papers, took a long pull on her drink, and then impulsively got up, went to the window, and wrapped herself in a drape.

"What do you think?" she asked Larry.

He had been sitting in the swivel chair at the desk. He looked up at her and suddenly there was naked lust in his eyes. You would have thought she had undressed rather than entwined herself in yards and yards of material. There wasn't anything of her showing except her head. For whatever reason, this had a powerfully aphrodisiac effect on Larry. He rose from the chair and took her, drape and all, into his arms. Theory collapsed before reality. Andrea not only did not resist, she continued in the manner of the flirtatious persona she had adopted and, when Larry hesitated after they had moved to the red leather couch, she took charge. A moral assessment of that first time would have been difficult. Who was seducer and who seducee? Larry, of course, claimed the lion's share of guilt.

She should have been prepared for his gargantuan remorse.

He sat on the edge of the couch, hands hanging between his knees, head bowed, a picture of dejection and despair. He had loved it, and it had been nice, very nice, but that counted against rather than for. Besides, he was now in a state of mortal sin; if he should die he would go straight to hell. It was only his own fate that anguished him. He claimed he could not rest until he had been to confession.

"Speaking of rest..." Andrea said.

They went upstairs to bed. If Larry was already damned, he might just as well take advantage of it and let her spend the night with him.

Her remorse came later and it was at her pliability during the episode. She tried to concentrate on the fact that, at the crucial point when they got to the couch, he would have stopped if she had let him, but all that proved was that she was as eager as Clare to do his bidding. They both overcame their separate remorses, she and Larry, and Andrea developed another theory. She was the New Woman cynically taking her pleasure with Larry and prepared to drop him as soon as he became an inconvenience or a bore. Became a bore! Dear God, it was his middle name. Whatever wit and grace and intelligence Larry had were drained from him while he was on the air. By the time he eluded Clare and came to her, he was a dull and weary man who sought and needed solace from her. The fact that he regarded every occasion as equivalent to damnation did not add to their cheerfulness, though it did seem to make him more zestful.

Had Clare been deceived? There had been times when Andrea wondered, but her estimate of Clare enabled her to dismiss the conjecture. Clare, as Andrea imagined her to be, would have a breakdown; indeed, do what eventually she did do, seek out a priest, tell him the whole dreadful story, and then take her own life.

It was clear that Clare had been deceiving them as much as they had been deceiving her. The whole concept of her rival had to be revised, beginning from the acceptance of an old girl friend as the reason for the Florida trip that marked the real beginning of things. Father Dowling's startling news about Clare's rendezvous in Fox River had first amused Andrea — the slyboots — but by the time she turned off the Interstate into Waukegan, she was feeling the annoyance of one who has been trifled with. There was the awful thought that during all those months when she had been feeling condescension toward Clare, Clare might have been feeling amused contempt toward her. Which of them, after all, was the liberated woman? She found she was glad Father Hogan's presence prevented her from bringing up the topic now.

"What do you say to the Pancake House?" Hogan asked brightly, sitting forward, pushing his head between hers and Larry's. Dinner at the Pancake House was Hogan's idea of a real treat.

"Good idea," Larry burbled. "Okay, Andrea?"

"Not for me. I have an appointment." With herself; she just wanted to get away from these two. "I can drop you there or swing by the house so you can pick up your car."

"We'll take a cab from there," Hogan said grandly, as if the streets of Waukegan crawled with taxis.

At the Pancake House, they hopped out of the car as happy as schoolboys. Watching them go, Andrea felt a bit like a cabbie herself. Oh, to hell with it. Home again, home again, jiggity jog.

Jack, Junior was waiting for her, sitting in a rented car at the curb. Once she would have thought it a defect that she felt so little natural tenderness toward her son, but now she saw him as half a stranger and knew he was a pompous moralistic ass. His general manner toward her was that of Torquemada: in a sane time she would have been burned at the stake for what she had done to Jack. He came toward her, suit coat flung over one shoulder, hair tousled, a sardonic smile. He was good looking, she admitted, damned good looking. A lot like his father at that age.

"What on earth brings you to Waukegan?"

"Would seeing my old Mom count as a reason?"

"Come on in. I'm dead tired. And please, no badinage. I've had a hell of a day."

"In Fox River?"

She turned from unlocking the door. The sun low in the west sent rays like laser beams low over the houses and Jack, Junior took on a roseate hue.

"You called my office." There was no reason why Nan shouldn't tell Andrea's own son where she was for the afternoon, but she did not like it. Jack, Junior was shaking his head, smile gone.

"No. I knew it was only a matter of time."

She hadn't the faintest idea what he was talking about. She certainly did not intend to solve the enigma on the doorstep. She opened the door and they went inside. She indicated the liquor.

"Make us a drink."

"Dad quit."

Dear God. Another ascetic. She went on into her room to get into something comfortable. She was surprised, when she emerged from the closet, to find Jack, Junior standing in the door of her room. He held out a gin and tonic.

"That all right?"

"Aren't you having anything?"

"Just some tonic water."

They went back into the living room, where she slumped into a chair and tasted her drink. "Mmmmm. Sit down, you make me nervous."

"Aren't you already?"

"What are you trying to say?"

"Have they identified him yet?"

"Who?"

"Dad."

"Jack, what in hell are you talking about?"

"Have the police found out yet that it was Dad whom Clare O'Leary went to see in Fox River?"

Andrea's mouth literally hung open. To say she was stunned would have been like saying that Archimedes was amused when he discovered the displacement of water. It was like hearing that the pope had decided to leave the priesthood. Jack! She started to laugh and found she could not, so awful was the expression on her son's face when she started.

"Don't," he advised, and his voice was arctic cold. "Don't."

"Jack, I just don't believe it. It's too incredible."

"Is it? I guess I stopped finding things incredible some time ago."

The old needle. Well, why not? In his place she would have felt the same way. But then her decision had been to occupy her own place, not someone else's. She hadn't expected applause and she could live with her family's condemnation. A first fugitive thought was that her son's remark was a new ploy on the part of Jack and the kids to get her to come to her senses. Just Molly and Me — "You'll learn to cook and to sew, what's more you'll love it, I know." One of Larry's golden oldies.

"He did it as a kind of revenge, I suppose." He looked at his glass of tonic water; it might have been hemlock. "They both did. That's why they got together in the first place. They had a common problem. You."

"Jack and Clare." He was right: it wasn't incredible. Clare. Andrea's memory was making a mad scan of the past several months and nothing conflicted with the thesis that Clare had somehow gotten in touch with her former husband. It would have been like the two of them, promising a kind of symmetry and balance. Justice served. And Clare would have found Jack distinguished. And, of course, he had money, the ultimate aphrodisiac. Andrea felt she had been betrayed.

"Was he with her there last week?"

He nodded. His expression said it all. What had been a silly, perhaps vindictive affair had turned into something else because Clare was dead. And so was that entertainer, Twinkie. My God! For the first time she understood the despair in her son's eyes. Jack?

Her first thought was: how can I protect him? Like her son, she did not find it incredible to think that Jack had been responsible for the death of Twinkie Zeugner.

20

THEY WERE lucky the room had not been cleaned. Horvath had every used glass and ashtray and towel bagged and labeled and sent to the lab. He wanted every print they could lift and whatever other identifiable signs of human use they could come up with. The speed with which Maxwell had gotten out of the High-Rise suggested they were going to have to prove he had ever been there. The glasses didn't look as if they had been wiped, so the chances were good they could establish Maxwell's residency.

"What do we have if we have that?" Agnes Lamb asked. She stood in the sitting room of the suite Maxwell had occupied and looked around with a mixture of admiration and disdain. "Imagine paying a month's rent to stay here one night."

"It's probably a business expense," Horvath said.

"And we know the kind of business he was in."

They did know, more or less. It was inconceivable that the traffic at the Stagecoach Inn was going on without Maxwell's knowledge and even less conceivable that it could continue without the blessing of the bosses who claimed Fox River as their territory.

"Maybe Zeugner didn't understand that."

"A little free-lancing on the side?"

Agnes shook her head. "From what I hear, he was strictly a buyer, not a seller."

"What did he get paid for playing the piano?"

"Ganser says five hundred a week." She avoided his eyes. It was embarrassing to think that someone who played old tunes by ear for several hours every night earned more than a cop, even one who had been around as long as Horvath.

"That's not nearly enough for the habit he had."

"Maybe it was a fringe benefit."

"That could give us a way to get Maxwell."

They might have been playing a game. Going after Maxwell was not exactly the order of the day, but Agnes had spent a lot of time around the Stagecoach and regarded talk about Clare O'Leary's boy friend as diversionary. She wanted to get those who had decided Hilda was a risk they need not run and then had gotten rid of her.

"Unless you subscribe to the suicide epidemic theory," she said half-tauntingly.

Well, she didn't have to convince Cy Horvath. He thought they had three related killings; Clare O'Leary, Twinkie Zeugner, and Hilda.

"I like the way we pulled all stops to find out what really happened to Hilda."

"Both of them looked like suicides, Agnes."

"Sure. Except for the fact that Hilda had never taken a drink in her life and Clare O'Leary had a fixation about not taking sleeping pills. And she's found full of sleeping pills and cocaine."

"What does the register of the Stagecoach tell us about Clare's boy friend?"

"Oh, she had one all right. The fact that they computerize room registration is a big help. We simply asked for the names of all those who had been staying in the motel on her previous visits. There were always two others there at the same time."

"Two?"

"One was Twinkie Zeugner. Computers aren't smart, only accurate. We asked a literal question and we got a literal answer."

"There was another man?"

"Yes."

"And he was there last week too, the day she died?"

"He was there."

"What do we know about him?"

"He had registered as J. F. Kinton each time he stayed at the Stagecoach, at least when he was there at the same time as Mrs. O'Leary. 'J.F.K.,'" Agnes mused. "Knowing the significance of those initials could be a clue to his age. A young man might think they stand for an airport."

"If he knows about the airport he knows about President Kennedy."

"Miss Muscles was vague on his age and what he looked like." That had been a worry, that Wilma, out of loyalty or love or whatever, had invented a boy friend for Clare O'Leary in order to keep her own memories of Twinkie intact. The way Keegan had described her giving the story had not inspired a lot of confidence. Keegan referred to Wilma Goudge as "the weightlifter." Did he resent the fact that she would only talk to him in the St. Hilary rectory?

"So check it out, Cy," Keegan had said, as if it were just routine. Agnes had thought it worse than routine until the computer turned up J.F.K.

Before going in from the parking lot, they decided to take on Ganser together and really work him over. It helped that the manager refused to see them when they asked for him at the desk. Horvath rounded the desk and pushed into the office unannounced.

Ganser had been turned away from the door. At the sound of it opening, he swung around, his eyes widening at the sight of Horvath. He sprang from the chair and made a doomed effort to get into his private bathroom with the thing he was smoking. Agnes Lamb closed the door behind her, shut her eyes, and inhaled through her nose. "Well, well," she said.

Horvath had grabbed Ganser's arm when he tried to get past him to the bathroom. Now he forcefully moved him back to the swivel chair behind the desk.

"I'll get you for illegal trespass," Ganser sputtered. "This is illegal. You can't come breaking in here like this."

"Where is a cop when you need one?" Agnes sighed.

"Better add false arrest, Ganser," Cy advised. "Officer Lamb, confiscate the evidence."

Ganser had not yet sat down. He looked at the burning roach in his hand. He might have been considering whether or not to swallow it. Finally he stubbed it out in his ashtray, mixing it up with the cigarette ashes and butts already there. Then he sat down and glared defiantly at Horvath.

"It's your word against mine."

"Then you're in trouble, Ganser. We suspected you were an addict..."

"I am not an addict! Good God, I just tried out a little grass to see what it was like and you come bursting in. Is that a capital crime?"

"It is when you're presiding over a zoo like the Stagecoach Inn. Drugs are available everywhere in this motel. I'm surprised you don't have them on the menu in the dining room."

"Funny," Ganser said.

Agnes had taken a chair in the corner. She spoke quietly. "While we're amusing you, Mr. Ganser, let me remind you of the three murders connected with this place."

He smiled and shook his head. "Don't bother to try. Two of those deaths are certified suicides and the third took place in another hotel."

"Where your boss was staying. Zeugner had gone over there, summoned by Maxwell. Maxwell told him he was through. Zeugner knew what that meant. He ditched the man who followed him from Maxwell's suite and a little later signed in at the High-Rise himself."

Ganser tried to look indifferent, but he was following this account with interest. Perhaps no one had bothered to tell him what had happened.

"He took a room at the High-Rise?"

"That's right."

"But he had a room here."

"Yes, but he thought if he returned to it, he might never leave it alive. Is that why you all become addicts, you're scared to death of getting killed?"

Ganser had to bite his tongue to refrain from charging at the red flag of the word "addict."

"Zeugner was not as stupid as the man Maxwell had sent after him. People like Maxwell are so lucky, aren't they? Finding others stupid enough to run their risks for them? Twinkie played the game as long as it was in his interest to play it. But he knew when the game was over and he made a good try at escaping."

"Some try!"

"Would you even try, Ganser? It's not just a theoretical question."

"Wait until Maxwell reads in the paper that the manager of his Fox River motel has been arrested for possession."

"It won't even matter if you get off."

"Maxwell might actually help you get off."

"Sure he will. He'll want you out where you can be tagged the way Twinkie was."

"I don't even know if Maxwell was in town," Ganser said.

"Didn't he get in touch? Well, why should he?"

"He was here to take care of Twinkie. Did you set Twinkie up, Ganser?"

He looked with hatred at Agnes. "I could never tell Twinkie what to do," he said to Horvath. "You know the size of the guy. If there was anyone I was afraid of, it was Zeugner."

"Why, did he ever hit you?"

"He wanted to, but he wasn't all that dumb."

"How dumb are you, Ganser?" Agnes asked. "You gonna sit here holding the bag for Maxwell?"

"There's no bag to hold."

"Then why did Maxwell clear out of town so fast?"

"I don't know that he was in town."

"Tell us about J.F.K.," Agnes said.

Ganser just looked at her, "J. F. Kinton," Horvath said. "He is one of your repeat customers."

"I don't know him."

"He was always in the motel when Mrs. O'Leary was here. Perhaps that will prod your memory."

Ganser shook his head. His eye drifted to the ashtray on his desk.

"You want to smoke, Ganser, go right ahead."

The manager fished a cigarette from the pack in the pocket of his shirt. It was hard to say whether he was more or less nervous than before.

"Do you know how many people stay here in the course of a week? It would be impossible to know them all."

"This man should have been at least as well-known to you as Clare O'Leary. You do remember Clare O'Leary, Ganser?"

"I do remember her."

"Good. It will be much better if you cooperate with us, Ganser. I can't promise you anything, but you stand a better chance of surviving than if you cover for Maxwell."

"Ha!" Ganser looked as if he wanted to cry.

"You're thinking of Zeugner? But he wasn't cooperating with us. Like the rest of you, he withheld information. None of you saw fit at first to mention that Mrs. O'Leary was a frequent guest at the motel."

"She had been here before."

"She was a guest who signed her own name, too. We need to know whether Kinton is J.F.K.'s real name. He gave an Atlanta home address every time but the first time he was here."

"I don't remember him."

"The first time he gave Tampa as his home town."

"Tampa, Florida," Agnes said.

"Doesn't remind me of a thing."

Agnes stood. "Okay. Shall we take him downtown, Lieutenant?"

Normally that would have been a bluff, but Cy sensed that Agnes saw here a chance to shake things up. If they were to bring Maxwell out of the woods, they had to do something like arrest Ganser.

"You've got to be kidding." Ganser sat forward. "Look, Horvath, you had me at a disadvantage when you broke in here. I admit that. You had your fun, so that's enough. You know and I know that you couldn't make a charge stick against me. You broke in here. I could have been doing a lot worse than I was and no judge is going to let that sort of case come to trial."

"That's interesting," Agnes said.

"You can explain it on the way downtown, Ganser. Come on, upsy-daisy."

Five minutes later they were heading for downtown with a Ganser who fluctuated from rage to hysteria. One way or another, arresting Ganser should start opening things up.

21

BREAD upon the waters, call it what you will, Tuttle had wondered when, if ever, something good would come his way from all the commotion surrounding the deaths of two women and one man. That disinterested friendly visit he had paid on Mervel the morning after Twinkie Zeugner had been mowed down in the lobby of the High-Rise was finally paying off. Mervel wanted Tuttle to represent him in his claims against Bruce Wiggins.

"He stole your stuff," Tuttle repeated thoughtfully. Let Mervel think Tuttle was making a swift mental review of the relevant law. The truth was, Tuttle was wondering if there *was* a significant body of law on the subject. Not that he hesitated to accept Mervel as a client. "When I'm done with Wiggins he won't have two dimes to rub together. By the way, you better give me something as a retainer."

"How much?"

"Just a symbolic sum. Do you have a hundred dollars?"

"A hundred dollars!"

"Any amount will do. Give me ten. Will the *Messenger* be joining you in this suit?"

"I never thought of that."

Tuttle pushed back his Irish hat and a wise little smile moved over his face like finger over dough. "That's what you have me for, Mervel."

If the *Messenger* came in on it, there would be a fee even in the quite likely event that Tuttle lost the suit. It was his principle that a case should always be conducted in such a way that his profit from it did not depend upon success. But, for all he knew, Mervel had a case.

"Tell me all about it."

Mervel looked at his watch. They were at the bar of the Fox Tail. Mervel must have known soberer moments, but that would have been years before. There was no point in dwelling on the likelihood that he owed his client and case to the rum and Cokes Mervel had been drinking.

"Rum and Coke is not a real drink, Tuttle. It is on the order of near beer. You can keep your hand in with it until the time comes for serious drinking. I should get over to Robertson's news conference."

"I was planning on going myself," Tuttle said breezily, though this was the first he had heard of a news conference by the Chief of Police.

Mervel slid from his stool, stood for a moment securing the floor beneath his feet, and began to move very rapidly toward the door, as if the floor were slanted. Who was it who said that walking is only arrested falling down? The definition captured Mervel's gait perfectly. Outside, the reporter gulped fresh air.

"What do you suppose Robertson will have to say?" Tuttle asked as they moved up the walk, seemingly against the flow of pedestrian traffic.

"He will apologize because the police are doing their job."

That goddamn Peanuts, Tuttle thought. Why hadn't he gotten in touch? "Good old Robertson," he said aloud, hoping this would prompt Mervel to go on.

"The police ought to know they can't arrest the manager of the Stagecoach Inn. Robertson knows."

"Ganser! What the hell happened?"

"I thought you knew."

"Only in general terms."

After he had the story, Tuttle was no longer surprised that

Peanuts had not called him about this one. It involved too intimately the Pianone turf. Tuttle was not sure it would be healthy for him to show up for the press conference. Who would believe he was attending with a client?

The press conference had been scheduled for the main lobby of the courthouse but someone persuaded Robertson that it would be wiser to have it somewhere small enough so that it did not appear he was being boycotted.

"Two papers, one shoppers' guide, and a rinky-dink television station, and he wanted to meet the press in a warehouse. Where did they find Robertson anyway, Tuttle?"

On a different occasion Tuttle might have defended Robertson. But it was another rule that one should adopt the outlook of the client, the better to get his angle on the case.

"He flunked out of the meter-maid academy," Tuttle said.

He was surprised by Mervel's roar of laughter. The man sounded drunk. Small wonder. All Tuttle knew was that Robertson had friends and those friends included the Pianone family. He could be Chief of Police as long as they wanted him to be.

Tuttle was all for going up the wide curving staircase that gave one such a fine panoramic view of the courthouse lobby, but Mervel shook his head, eyes closed. So they got into one of the turn-of-the-century elevators, a wrought-iron cage that rose up a greased pole and should have been condemned years ago. The view from the elevators was better than from the staircase, if your heart wasn't in your throat, that is. Tuttle thought it compromised the dignity of the courthouse to have this amusement-park ride in it.

"I don't trust elevators," Mervel said.

"We should have walked." Tuttle did not have his eyes shut but he willed them not to record anything.

"I had a teacher named Otis. Miss Otis." Mervel shivered.

The conference had been moved to Robertson's outer office. Wiggins and his crew had already set up, and the bright lights brought out the cracks and stains on the walls. Mervel growled at the sight of the TV newsman. Wiggins, seeing them come in, advanced on them with a winning smile.

"Mervel," he cried. "What is this about a law suit?"

Tuttle interposed himself between the television and newspaper reporters.

"As counsel for Mr. Mervel and the other principals, I have advised him not to discuss the case."

"Who the hell are you?"

"Tuttle, the lawyer. Senior partner at Tuttle and Tuttle. I have a card here somewhere." Tuttle took off his hat and looked inside it.

"Don't bother. Is this true, Mervel? You won't talk to me?"

"I'm afraid you might steal anything I say."

"That's libel," Wiggins cried. He grabbed Tuttle's arm. "You heard him. You're a witness."

Tuttle smiled. "Haven't you heard of the sacred lawyer/client relationship?"

This came to an end when Robertson burst from his inner office. Apparently he had been misinformed. He looked at the handful of people in his outer office and could not keep disappointment from his face. He looked as if he wanted to turn right around and disappear. But he was pushed from behind. He went to a table on which a small lectern had been placed and took a piece of paper from his pocket.

"I have a prepared statement. After I have read it, I'll take questions."

"Can't you just distribute it?" Maud from the Shoppers' Guide asked querulously.

"Read it, Chief," Wiggins directed, and Robertson did. "'On advice of the city attorney, I am making a public statement about an arrest made earlier today by two officers of the detective division of the Fox River Police Department. Mr. William Ganser, Manager of the Stagecoach Inn, was taken from his office to police headquarters under the mistaken impression that he had broken a law. The manner in which this was done, according to the city attorney, left nearly everything to be desired. Consequently, I am making a public apology to Mr. Ganser on behalf of the Police Department.'"

Robertson put the paper back in his pocket and began to turn.

"Chief, we didn't get it all. Could you read it again for the camera?"

Robertson nodded to Wiggins. "Of course." He accepted Wiggins's implication that the event had not really transpired until it was recorded on film.

"To hell with that, Chief," Mervel said. "Who arrested Ganser?"

"Those names will not be given out at this time."

"Pending notification of next of kin?" Maud grinned at Robertson.

"What did the arresting officers think Ganser was guilty of?"

"We're trying to forget that, not continue it."

"Is this public apology part of some deal, Chief?"

"What are you doing here, Tuttle?"

"Is it a deal?" Mervel demanded.

"All I will say is that I am acting on the advice of the city attorney."

22

IT WAS the kind of speculation Phil Keegan was not completely at ease discussing with Father Dowling.

From being a puzzling suicide, the death of Clare O'Leary had become an episode in a far larger series of events that Keegan could not quite make out through the haze. The woman who had convinced Roger Dowling she was a victim of marital woes suddenly had connections all over the place, and none of them did much to preserve the image she had tried to create when she visited the St. Hilary rectory.

The priest ran a finger down the line of his thin nose. "It was like a bad confession."

"How do you mean?"

"Sometimes people confess to a few peccadilloes, concealing serious sins, thinking the absolution they receive covers everything. Maybe Clare O'Leary was seeking carte blanche by calling on a strange priest."

Phil Keegan thought this far-fetched. "Well, we know why she came to Fox River. The suggestion that she just happened to stop at the Stagecoach was a bunch of malarkey. Is there any part of her story that hasn't been disproved by the facts?"

"She said her husband was having an affair with his lawyer."

Keegan ignored that. "First, we find out that she and that piano player, Zeugner, were apparently up to something. Then he's killed."

"But not by her."

"Not by her." It was best to remain patient and calm when Roger Dowling got into this mood. The pastor of St. Hilary seemed to think he was obliged to defend the good name of the woman who had come to the rectory and lied to him. It was not like Roger to nit-pick like that. "I meant we have other evidence."

"But evidence of what, Phil? Zeugner was a user and Harley was a dealer."

"Clare O'Leary had been using drugs the day she died. She had stayed at the Stagecoach before. It seems pretty clear she went there to be able to buy the stuff."

"From Zeugner?"

"That's the way it looks."

"So there need not have been any romantic dalliance between the two."

"Maybe not. But the muscle woman from the Stagecoach says there was another guy she used to meet at the Stagecoach. This was a very busy lady, Roger."

"No wonder her husband threatened to have her killed."

Keegan shook his head. "Forget all the romantic stuff, Roger. What we very probably have here is a territorial dispute. Zeugner tried to play it cute and paid the price."

"If you think Maxwell is responsible, you should arrest him."

Roger Dowling as irate taxpayer? In this mess anything was possible. Keegan felt a little less than honest, acting as if only Dowling was puzzled by what had happened. But Keegan did not want his old friend to start nagging him. Agnes Lamb was bad enough.

Lamb acted as if Keegan was engaged in some great coverup lest the murderer of Hilda, the Stagecoach maid, be found.

"What's the connection with Hilda?"

"Maybe there isn't one. Her sister Gloria is a maid at the Sleepytime where Harley was killed."

"Yes?"

"I don't know what the connection is, but there must be one."

It didn't speak well for Lamb's future as a cop if she was going to make leaps and jumps like that and insist she was simply moving from A to B. Agnes seemed to think there was something racial going on, and Keegan could not for the life of him see what it was.

"They killed Hilda," Agnes said.

"She was found dead in her car."

"Sure. And Clare O'Leary was found dead in her motel room."

"Keep on it," Keegan told her.

"Lamb will turn it up if there's anything to turn up," Cy assured him.

Horvath's confidence in Lamb was touching, but in this instance it wasn't quite justified. At least not yet. Keegan told himself to keep an open mind. If Lamb found something he would sure act on it. At least Agnes Lamb was looking for a connection with the Fox River drug traffic. Which is where they were going to find an explanation of Zeugner's murder. And of Clare O'Leary's death, if it needed an explanation.

"Are you going back to suicide, Phil?" Roger Dowling asked.

"She died of an overdose of sleeping tablets."

"Her husband said she had never taken a sleeping tablet in her life."

"Sure, and she said he was out to kill her."

"That sounds more plausible rather than less, doesn't it, Phil? If she was up to half the shenanigans people say she was, that provides a powerful motive to her husband."

"He was on the radio in Waukegan at the time his wife died."

"He never said he would do it himself."

"Maybe he hired J. F. Kinton to do it."

"Have you found out who he is?"

Keegan shook his head. "The fact that he was here on the same dates as the O'Leary woman doesn't establish anything."

"Was he ever at the Stagecoach when she wasn't there?"

"No. And he never stayed in any other local hotel. Or motel. What's more, if he exists, the Internal Revenue and Social Security people have never heard of him."

"The use of an alias makes him interesting, doesn't it?"

"Not at a place like the Stagecoach."

Roger, who had been busy filling and lighting his pipe, opened the drawer of his desk and brought out a deck of cards. It was one of those rare occasions when there was no game worth watching on television. So far as Keegan could tell, only sports drew Roger Dowling to the television set. The priest made a face when Keegan asked him if he watched the news.

"I get the feeling that it's watching me, Phil."

Dowling preferred the news in print. He certainly was a diligent reader of the Chicago papers as well as of the Fox River *Messenger*.

"Mervel is keeping a close eye on you this time, Phil. I suppose being a witness to a slaying adds a note of urgency to reporting."

"He's crazy. Do you know he's hired Tuttle as his lawyer?"

"I didn't even know he'd been arrested."

"Ho ho. I gather he's thinking of suing someone."

Dowling gave Keegan the cards to shuffle while he set up the little table between the two easy chairs in the rectory study.

"Do you need a fresh beer, Phil?"

"Thanks."

Whatever testiness there had been was gone. Keegan poured what beer remained in his bottle and gave the empty to Roger. Two old friends about to have a friendly game of pinochle. He wished he could placate Agnes Lamb and Mervel and his other critics as easily.

If Roger Dowling was indeed placated.

23

THE ROBERTSON news conference, which he had attended in the company of his more or less lawyer, Tuttle, had snapped Mervel out of it and he meant to stay snapped out of it. A way of vindicating all the lost years seemed to stretch before him and he meant to take it. It was Tuttle's mention of Milwaukee that triggered the realization that there was one whole unexplored side of the deaths of Twinkie Zeugner, Hilda, and Clare O'Leary.

"You mean Waukegan," Mervel said, cutting into Tuttle's babble when they had left the press conference and were headed for the Fox Tail lounge.

"No. Milwaukee. Where she came from, the lawyer, Andrea Kohler. Not that it matters. Anyway..."

"How long ago?"

"How long ago what?"

"Did she come from Milwaukee?"

Tuttle's nose seemed to touch the brim of his hat. He was thinking. He shrugged. "I seem to remember a couple of years ago."

"Did she practice in Milwaukee?"

"Geez! I don't know. Who cares?"

It was a sense Mervel had not had for some years, a hunch that something being systematically overlooked was the important thing and he alone recognized it. Hunches such as this distinguish good reporters from bad, and Mervel had not had more than one or two such hunches in his career. Maybe that is why this one struck him so forcefully.

In the Fox Tail lounge he ordered a beer.

"Have a shot with that," Tuttle advised.

"Not this morning."

"Going back to bed? I noticed you haven't shaved."

But drinking nothing stronger than beer was a bet he made with himself, as if a little asceticism would earn him the happy outcome of pursuing his hunch. He had only two beers, said "So long" to Tuttle, and then went home and shaved. The thought of catching a few hours' sack time was powerfully attractive, but Mervel squared his shoulders. It was Milwaukee or bust. Perhaps one way or the other. But his hunch was even stronger than before. This would be a turning point in his career, no doubt of it. Let Wiggins eat his heart out.

It was late morning when Mervel wheeled his ten-year-old import onto the Interstate and pointed its tinny nose north toward Milwaukee. He was almost surprised to see how heavy the traffic was. It was as if the business of the world had been going on unnoticed by him for years. And he was in the news business. He felt vaguely ashamed, and the redemptive promise of this trip was all the more attractive. Andrea Kohler was the key, Mervel was sure of it. He didn't know how, but he was sure. This trip to Milwaukee would tell him how.

Of course it was easier to think that all that was involved here was the mob and drugs and that the bodies found in Fox River were just a little mopping up to keep the traffic clean. Like most successful businessmen, the mob really didn't believe in a free market, supply and demand, that sort of crap. They wanted a monopoly and the ability to raise prices as they saw fit. From that perspective, Zeugner could be accounted for and the O'Leary woman written off as someone who had been caught up in something rougher than she had imagined.

The added attraction of this explanation was that it ended the matter. No one was likely to run the risk of learning too much about underworld operations. The federal government maybe could afford to run the risk, but not the local, certainly not the Fox River police force, not with Robertson as chief. And not the Fox River *Messenger* either.

It was too easy to be mesmerized by an explanation that could never really be tested. But what if they were all looking in the wrong direction? An old journalism professor had insisted there are only two major sources of the event that earn the name of news — sex and money. If money was ruled out, that left sex, and what was needed was someone with sufficient motive to take care of Zeugner and Clare O'Leary. Larry O'Leary? He was the obvious candidate, of course, and that phony foundation as memorial for his wife, Wiggins's sycophantic coverage of it, suggesting that, like all television performers, Larry O'Leary was the soul of generosity — all that made Mervel want to come up with decisive proof that the Waukegan king of the airwaves was responsible for both his wife's and Twinkie Zeugner's deaths.

O'Leary as J.F.K.? The idea had an absurdity that commended it, when you thought of O'Leary. The assumption was that J.F.K. came to meet Clare O'Leary, and of course it was crazy to suppose O'Leary had to set up a rendezvous with his own wife. But think of him at the motel in the role of spy and everything changed. O'Leary would be a rare show-business type if the thought of dressing up and disguising himself did not appeal to him.

And that is when the crazy, mad, incredible, yet irresistible, hunch about Andrea Kohler came to him.

What if J.F.K. was Andrea Kohler? Having those two beers with Tuttle in the Fox Tail, Mervel actually avoided the lawyer's eyes, fearful that his nutty surmise about Andrea Kohler would somehow leak out of his own and bring a derisive hoot from the little lawyer. To neutralize the possibility, he asked Tuttle his opinion of Andrea Kohler.

"Professionally?" Tuttle pinched his upper lip between thumb and forefinger. Was he remembering the close calls he had had with the bar association? "I have to give her points for the way she protects her client when they come to town. I think the only one who has managed to talk with O'Leary without her being present is Father Dowling. Otherwise she's been right there, making sure he doesn't say anything stupid."

And incriminating. "You looked into O'Leary's foundation?"

"That's another thing. She discouraged it, she is delaying it. The guy really seems moved by some guilty desire to throw his money away."

Mervel did not pursue it. Now, holding to a middle lane on the Interstate, with enormous trucks roaring by to his right and cars flashing past him to his left, it was difficult to think at all. If anyone on the Interstate had heard of the 55 MPH speed limit they gave no indication of it. The only warning that bothered Mervel was the 45 MPH minimum speed. He hoped he could keep his heap up to that.

At the *Journal* he was given some barely tolerant help (the Fox River *Messenger*?), but it was help, and toward mid-afternoon he found himself in a rectangular office on the nineteenth floor of a downtown building, seated across the desk from Dr. Alexander Howell. With the blades of light from the tilted blind lying on him, the counselor looked like the subject of an art photograph. Howell was bald but had a massive mustache, the corners of which he twitched rhythmically. He was a laicized Jesuit who had known Andrea when she lived in Milwaukee.

"Not well. But she came to see me at the time of the divorce." Howell lit a cigarette and sent a cloud of smoke through the chiaroscuro air. "She took it a lot better than John did, but his attitude made it difficult for her. I helped her through it, I think I can say. There was no reason why she should pay for his unresolved conflicts."

"You told her to get a divorce?"

"She already intended to get a divorce. I would not have

told her to do one thing as opposed to another in any case. That is not the way counseling works." Howell's tolerant smile reminded Mervel of the reception he had received at the *Journal*.

"You just agree with the client?"

Howell put out his cigarette. "What is your interest in the Kohlers?"

"His first name was John?"

Even before Howell answered, Mervel saw in a flash what his hunch had been a hunch about. John Kohler. And his middle initial would be F. Mervel would have bet a month's salary on it. He got abruptly to his feet. This put Howell at a disadvantage.

"John Kohler. Yes. Has anything happened to Andrea?"

"Maybe she'll contact you," Mervel said.

Going down in the elevator, he found himself resenting Howell, sitting in his shaded office in affluent spendor. Men who left the ministry ought to go to work. Mervel was not a religious man, but he had severe views on how ministers and priests should comport themselves. He was capable of shock when he saw a minister in anything other than a compact car; he nodded sagely whenever it was suggested that most religious work was just a racket to raise money. But cynical as his professed views might be, Mervel subconsciously wanted the clergy to act like St. Francis or Mahatma Ghandi. It shocked him to think of a former Jesuit encouraging a woman to get a divorce.

There was no J. F. Kohler in the phone directory and Mervel regretted having left Howell's office as he had. Back to the *Journal* he went. There was an old story on Andrea, in her Junior League days. A more recent one covered her graduation from law school (Mother of Three Takes Law Degree). And then he found the item he sought. J. F. Kohler, long an engineer in this city, was moving to the Tampa-St. Petersburg region to live a life of semiretirement. He and his son would continue the family business in Florida.

Mervel returned to Fox River by lesser roads, not wanting the terror of the Interstate to stop the flow of speculation. If Andrea's husband was the J. F. Kinton who had stayed at the Stagecoach when Clare O'Leary was there, where did that really take things? If Larry O'Leary and his lawyer were having an affair, as Tuttle suggested, then *they* should have been the objects of jealous rage, Andrea of her estranged husband's, Larry of Clare's. Clare might have been knocked off to smooth the way for Andrea and Larry, but surely Andrea's old husband would not do the two of them that kind of favor.

No matter how he turned the facts, no matter the combinations he tried to force them into, Mervel could make no sense of them. But he was not discouraged. He had discovered a very significant piece of the puzzle, there was no doubt about that. It wasn't important that he himself was unable immediately to solve the puzzle itself.

But if not he, who? All he had to do was imagine discussing what he had learned with Tuttle to sense that would be absurd. It occurred to him that he hadn't had a drink since those beers with Tuttle before lunch. Did he mean to give up drink until he had followed through on the great lead he had hit on? The thought of such abstinence turned his thoughts to Roger Dowling. From Howell to Dowling. That made some sort of sense, he was not sure how. But Roger Dowling was someone he could talk to without worrying about losing the value of his discovery.

24

"DID YOU get a photograph of John F. Kohler?" Roger Dowling asked.

Mervel sat at the dining room table, a cup of coffee and a piece of cherry pie before him. Mrs. Murkin lingered in the doorway. The reporter had refused a meal, having arrived just as Roger Dowling was finishing his. The housekeeper would have been reluctant to go to great trouble for this guest, a man who had not always been friendly to the pastor of St. Hilary's, yet she seemed somewhat miffed that he had refused the meal. Coffee and dessert were an honorable compromise, however, and eventually Marie Murkin withdrew to her kitchen.

"It's several years old and posed. The *Journal* used the cut several times over a five-year period, the last time more than five years ago."

"He can't have changed radically, not at this time of his life."

Mervel looked up from his rapidly disappearing pie, a bit like the student who has not heard the question.

"Have you spoken to anyone else about this, Mr. Mervel?"

A vigorous shake of the head. "I came right here."

"Why?"

Mervel pushed his plate away, sipped his coffee, and put the cup very carefully back into its saucer. "That's hard to say. I wanted to talk about it, but confidentially. I know you know

Keegan and follow his investigations as closely as anyone. First, I've hit on something very important, don't you agree?"

"It certainly seems to be."

"So how do I proceed? The simplest thing would be to turn it over to Keegan, but as soon as I do that every other journalist has as much right to the story as I do. That isn't fair."

"But you have to learn whether you have really discovered something."

"You mean, give it to Keegan?" Mervel looked sad, almost betrayed.

On the wall behind Mervel hung a painting of the Last Supper, one of Roger Dowling's few mementos of the home in which he had been raised. Even as a boy, Dowling had been fascinated and repelled by the depiction of Judas in the painting, at the end of the table, looking away from Jesus, his face twisted in despair. The betrayer. Roger Dowling would have preferred to be looking at something else while he in effect counseled Mervel to bypass the police, at least for the moment. Of course he did this as obliquely as Howell might have in his prime.

"What the police would do is take the photograph to the Stagecoach and see if they could get an identification." Roger Dowling puffed on his pipe.

"Ganser is pretty fed up with the whole business. I probably couldn't get in to see him. And, if he found out I was·asking around, he would have me run out of there."

"Do you know Miss Wilma Goudge, the woman who is in charge of the physical fitness center at the Stagecoach?"

It seemed only right that he should put Mervel into contact with the person who had told him of the man Clare O'Leary had come to the Stagecoach to meet. That mysterious man from out of town could very well be the former husband of Andrea Kohler.

"What if it is?" Mervel asked.

"Let's cross that bridge when we come to it."

The trite remark seemed to reassure Mervel. Roger Dowling

had wondered if the reporter saw how puzzling it would be if it had indeed been Andrea's husband who was at the Stagecoach at the same time as Clare, there to meet her, if Wilma Goudge was to be believed. If true, this would do little toward explaining Clare O'Leary's death. A falling out of lovers? But this was to pile conjecture on top of conjecture. Nothing that had been learned from interrogating the help at the Stagecoach suggested any basis for such speculation. Of course, as Phil Keegan remarked somewhat bitterly, the employees at the Stagecoach were the least helpful bunch the Fox River police had questioned in years.

"More coffee?"

"No thanks, Father."

"Would you care for a drink?"

Roger Dowling immediately regretted the question. The moral struggle that was reflected on Mervel's narrow face was one the pastor of St. Hilary's had not wished to occasion.

"I wouldn't mind a beer," Mervel said in a thin voice.

There was no beer in the refrigerator. Marie Murkin's announcement of this, coming on the heels of Mervel's lost argument with himself, seemed some sort of white lie. Roger Dowling went into the kitchen himself and verified Mrs. Murkin's claim while she looked on nonplused.

"It doesn't matter, Father." Mervel had come into the kitchen too. Suddenly he had the buoyancy of one who has just performed an heroic deed. "Besides, I better get going on what we talked about."

"You're going to do that right away, tonight?"

"What's the point of waiting?" Mervel might have been procrastination's greatest foe.

"Do you think I'm hiding beer or something?" Mrs. Murkin said plaintively when the reporter was gone.

"It's a long story."

"That man will think you have a housekeeper who drinks up all the beer herself."

"I'm sorry, Marie."

On another occasion he might have teased her because of her reaction, but not tonight. Mervel had indeed stumbled on something fascinating.

"I can go get beer," Mrs. Murkin said.

"That isn't necessary, Marie. Don't be silly."

"What if Captain Keegan decides to come?"

"If he does, we'll worry about beer then."

It would have been too much to say that Marie Murkin had a premonition. The odds in favor of Phil Keegan's dropping by the St. Hilary rectory unannounced on a weekday evening were always high.

"There isn't any beer," Marie Murkin told him when she answered the door.

"Is Father Dowling in?"

"In the study. I'll run out for beer."

This odd greeting for their frequent guest brought Roger Dowling out of his study. "Marie, there is no need for you to be going to the store at this time of night." The flicker of disappointment on Phil's face prompted him to go on. "Captain Keegan and I will go."

It was a cool night with the smell of autumn in it so they decided to walk the five blocks to the twenty-four-hour grocerteria to buy the beer. On the way, Roger Dowling asked if there was any further news on Maxwell.

"I thought you were urging me to look into the mysterious J.F.K."

"Have you been?"

"With the kind of backing we get from Robertson, it's surprising I can get anyone to do anything. Lamb comes up with a thing like that and what can we do with it?"

On the way back to the rectory, the conversation turned to the Bears, scarcely a more cheerful topic, but the folly of the football team was not one Phil Keegan felt so directly implicated in that he could not derive some satisfaction from castigating it. He was still at it when the phone in the rectory study rang. It was Mervel.

"No soap, Father Dowling."

"Tell me about it," Roger Dowling said, allowing his eyes to drift over Phil Keegan's head in the hope that his old friend would surmise he was dealing with some spiritual problem.

"There's nothing to tell. I showed the picture to the woman in the gym and she said no." Mervel's voice sounded thick.

"I'm sorry to hear that."

"Oh, I might have known..." Mervel's tragic voice went quiet.

"It was a brilliant idea," Roger Dowling said.

"Sure. Well, I thought I'd let you know." There seemed to be the hum of voices in the background now. The sound of a bar. Poor Mervel.

"Thank you. I appreciate it." When he returned the phone to its cradle, Roger Dowling was tempted to tell Phil of Mervel's great idea and of its collapse. Even negative facts have their uses. But it seemed to put the reporter in a ridiculous light and Roger Dowling did not wish to add to Mervel's woes.

Shortly before two the following morning Roger Dowling came out of a sound sleep with a conviction every bit as exciting as Mervel's had been. Recalling the reporter at the dining room table telling how his hunch had come to him did nothing to diminish the excitement Roger Dowling felt. He tried to convince himself that it was one of those dead-of-night ideas destined to wither in the light of day. He assured himself that his notion, like Mervel's, was fated to be quickly disproved. But he didn't believe it for a minute. He eased his head back onto the pillow and whispered a prayer of thanksgiving for what seemed almost an inspiration.

In the morning, the idea seemed if possible more exciting. He was up with the birds — a favorite expression of his mother —

and his first thought was to telephone Mervel and include him in this variation of the reporter's hunch. But he decided against it. Despite his optimism, it was possible he was mistaken, and Mervel did not sound like a man who needed his hopes dashed twice on successive days. So at eight o'clock Roger Dowling set out alone for Waukegan.

He hoped to catch Andrea Kohler before she went to her office.

25

FOR THE first time, Andrea felt responsible for Clare O'Leary's death.

Jack, Junior's story, initially incredible, became all too quickly plausible. It was just the sort of irrationally vindictive thing Jack would do. And it was simon-pure male chauvinism.

In such a situation, the women did not really count. If they did, Jack would have revenged himself by acting directly against her. But he was no more able to take her seriously now when she was independent of him and had proved she could both take care of herself and excel at it, than he had been when she was part of the unnoticed background to his life. If something had gone wrong, the reason must be a man, and if anyone was to be punished, it had to be a man.

That meant, of course, that Clare herself had been a mere instrument of an essentially male exchange. It was all on the same moral level as letting the air out of the rival's tires, breaking his windows, fire bombing his garage. In this case, kill his wife. See how he likes it. Clare would not have entered into the reckoning at all, not in any serious sense.

These thoughts did not diminish Andrea's sense of guilt. Somehow she felt responsible for what had happened. And it did not help to tell herself how absurd this was. If she could be guilty of things over which she had as little control as what had happened in Fox River, the whole concept of responsibility was diluted beyond recognition. It was like one of those bull sessions in law school, over beer after moot court, when they had momentarily permitted themselves to acknowledge the wider significance of the law. Andrea knew which side of this one she would have been on in more academic circumstances and she had no doubt that in academic circumstances her side would have prevailed. There was no way in the world she could be held accountable for what Jack had done to Clare O'Leary.

And Twinkie Zeugner too? My God. If Clare, then Twinkie. It seemed to form itself like an argument in a brief. But why Twinkie?

Jack, Junior had been satisfied to see that she understood what he was saying and that she believed it.

"Where are you going?" she asked.

He stood by the opened front door, his hand on the knob. His expression was one of disgust faintly laced with pity.

"I'm a workingman, Mother. There is more to my life than cleaning up after my parents."

"Have you told anybody else about this?"

He laughed. "Just thank God this happened in a hick town where getting away with murder is not all that hard."

"But a police investigation is bound to turn up the fact that your father..."

Jack, Junior was shaking his head. He wore a solid navy-blue tie with a blue striped shirt. His topcoat was over one arm, his unbuttoned suit coat revealed his vest. Black loafers, tasseled, set off the gray-blue suit. He looked like a model in a catalogue. Was this her son? For a moment she saw him as strangers might, but then the familiar lens of the motherly relation was back and he was just Jack, Junior all dressed up and proposing to go.

"You just told me this so I'd know?"

"Call it a family secret."

He closed the door after him with a theatrical precision. From the window Andrea watched him get into the car parked in the driveway and back slowly into the street. He looked both ways, used the turn signal. He could have been giving lessons in driving. That is the kind of child he had been, meticulous, a perfectionist.

In Lent, as a boy, Jack, Junior drew up graphs on which he recorded the fidelity with which he performed the acts of penance he had set himself. The little boxes were filled in, more every day, like a crossword puzzle, the result seeming to call out for a gold star. There had been a time when Andrea was sure her son had a vocation, she even spoke to one of the priests who taught him. Jack was furious. Staunch Catholic that he was, he could not help but think of a priestly or religious vocation as a waste. No son of his was going to whisper his life away in some dim church heavy with the smell of wax and incense. Jack, Junior? He did what he was told. If they had sent him off to the Trappists, he would have gone off without a whimper. And now he was caught up in a drama so lurid it belonged in the tabloids. How could Jack do this to them?

But she could not succeed in transferring the guilt to Jack. Transferring? That is where it belonged. No matter. She found it all too easy, even after the years spent ridding herself of the propensity, to think that, if only she had remained a dutiful housewife, if only she hadn't reacted so strongly the night Jack told her to be quiet in front of company, if only... If the past had been different, the present would be different.

She spent a restless night. In the morning she got up at six, put on a very large pot of coffee, and drank three cups while trying to decide if she would go to the office today. She compromised and called in to say she would be late. "I'll be working at home," is the way she put it.

When Father Dowling arrived, Andrea had taken her coffee cup into the living room and was sitting sipping and felt both confused and frightened at the sound of the bell. Her first thought was that it was Jack, Junior returning, and she ran to the door in the mad hope that he would deny having told her all those dreadful things the night before. The sight of the priest angered her.

She did not want to see a priest. Roger Dowling might not be David Hogan, but he was a priest nonetheless. Any guilt she felt would only be increased by the sight of a Roman collar.

Curiosity dictated she open the door to him, that and professional decorum. The priest knew her as counsel for Larry and that seemed the only possible basis for his showing up on her doorstep.

"They told me you were working at home today."

"That's a bit of a euphemism, Father. The truth is I'm just vegetating. Could I give you a cup of coffee?"

"Please."

When she came back with it, he was leaning over, studying the framed photographs that stood on a table beside the couch.

"Your family?"

"Those pictures are very dated. Everyone has changed so much. Particularly my daughters."

"Do you see them much?" He took the coffee, black as he had wanted it, and sat. Such little *pro forma* questions about the family were the stock in trade of the visiting cleric. Everyone likes to talk of their kids. And, if they don't, the priest knows something is wrong.

"Not half as much as I'd like to. But they are raising their families now and are busy from dawn to dusk. As I so well remember."

"You have three children?" He glanced toward the photographs on the table.

"Two daughters, one son."

"He seems to favor you rather than his father."

"Jack, Junior? I suppose he does. Parents are usually surprised when people tell them who their children look like, have you noticed? Maybe we see them as so unique we can't accommodate the thought that they may be just a new edition of a familiar type."

"I only meant that I can't imagine anyone mistaking your son for your husband."

She stopped herself on the verge of correcting him. Ex-husband, former husband, not husband. But that would have invited an interminable theological squabble. "No, I guess not."

"What does he do?"

"Jack is semiretired. He and my son are both engineers. And they both live in Florida."

"Tampa?"

"How did you know that?"

"Statistically, the chances of someone from the Midwest living on the east coast of Florida are small. If they are in business, St. Petersburg or Tampa are far more likely than, say, Sarasota or Fort Myers."

"You seem to know Florida very well."

"Not at all. These are things I have read."

"Then you sound like a detective."

"The Fox River police don't seem to be making much progress in their investigation into the death of Clare O'Leary."

"I think they've gotten as far as they're likely to get. Frankly, they are not a very impressive group of people."

"They do have the J.F.K. initials to work on."

He said it casually, little or no emphasis in his voice, and he did not stare at her to surprise her in a revelatory reaction. She wanted desperately to think he had just made a random remark. But the very fact that it seemed so alarmed her. She made an impatient noise.

"Your husband's initials."

"Oh, for heaven's sake."

He looked at her and nodded. "Yes, it is a preposterous suggestion. No one at the motel recognizes a photograph of your husband. No one there ever saw him."

"How do you know that? Is that true?" She could not keep the delighted squeal from her voice.

"The idea was bound to occur to someone. It occurred to one of our local reporters. He managed to get hold of a photograph of your husband, with the negative results I've mentioned."

When she had come to after delivering, it had always been something of a disappointment not to feel smaller and lighter than she was. The sense of change, of having laid her burden down, came later, gradually. But now Father Dowling's words gave her the immediate sense of reprieve and of being returned to the *status quo ante* she had craved in the maternity ward.

"The thought must have occurred to you as well," he said.

Why lie? He must see how relieved she was. She nodded, lips pulled in, eyebrows raised, eyes shining.

"Did the other possibility also occur to you?"

"What do you mean?"

"Your son? Jack, Junior?"

It was not fair that she should be dashed so soon into anxious fear after the exhilaration of learning that Jack was not responsible for the death of Clare O'Leary. Who had suggested he was? Jack, Junior was avenging himself on both his parents in one fell blow. But this was worse, infinitely worse. Awful as it had been to think Jack had killed Clare, it was worse than awful to substitute her son for her husband.

"It couldn't have been Jack, Junior," she snapped at Father Dowling.

"When did you last see him?"

"He lives in Florida."

"So does your husband."

"It's different."

"Does your son ever come north?"

"He did not kill Clare O'Leary."

"Would he have wanted people to suspect his father?"

"No. My God, they were close as that. He went to live with his father after..."

"He disapproved of what you had done?"

"Of course he disapproved. Children always disapprove when their parents act like people."

"Andrea, this is how the police will question you. I don't

□ 155 □

have to tell you that. They will question your son as well. If they find he has been in Chicago on the dates when J.F.K. was registered at the Stagecoach Inn..."

"You mean you're going to tell them?"

"That isn't what I mean at all. The police are not stupid, nor are reporters. The reporter who thought J.F.K. was your husband is certain to think of your son, eventually."

"Accusations aren't enough. Indictments aren't enough."

And they weren't. The police could suspect Jack, Junior. They could gather evidence against him, circumstantial evidence. They could get an indictment, bring him to trial. That did not mean a conviction. The chances against a conviction were enormous. Andrea knew that. But these thoughts were not comforting. She could not think of her son simply in legal terms. The thought of the accusation even being made went through her like a knife.

"I want to talk to him, Andrea."

"Why?"

"I want to talk to him before the police do."

"And urge him to turn himself in?" she asked bitterly.

"I was thinking of another assessment of his deed, Andrea. Not the legal one."

He seemed almost embarrassed to have to remind her what his interest as a priest chiefly was. Souls. The saving of souls. Andrea had never been able to imagine a soul satisfactorily. She thought of vapor escaping the body or a ghostly *Doppelgänger* keeping in step. Priests were in the business of saving souls. Father Dowling was interested in her son's soul. But she could not care about that; she wanted to save him as he was, flesh and blood. She did not want him dragged into this awful mess and she did not care whether he was guilty or not. The streets are thronged with uncaught criminals.

"I can give you his address in Florida."

A small smile. "Can you give me another cup of coffee?"

He drank the second cup standing. The ordeal was over. Andrea wanted him out of the house so she could think. How on earth was she going to get in touch with Jack, Junior?

For a moment, while Father Dowling stood in the doorway, she thought he was going to give her a blessing. They had had the priest bless their home in New Berlin before moving in, she remembered. Obviously that blessing had not taken.

Fifteen minutes after the priest left, Jack, Junior was at the door. There was no car in the driveway and he did not look quite so dapper as he had the night before. He pushed past her into the house, pulling the door shut behind him.

"Who was that priest? Hogan?"

"He is from Fox River."

He looked at her narrowly, as if deciding whether to believe her.

"He is the priest Clare O'Leary visited just before she died."

"What did he want?"

"A reporter in Fox River figured out the significance of the initials. J.F.K."

He did not seem to know whether to be horrified or pleased.

"He also had the intelligence to show people at the motel a picture of your father."

"And?"

"You know what the result of that was."

A smile broke over his face. "Then he isn't in any trouble?"

"No. You are."

He snorted. "Are you going to turn me in?"

"How long do you think it will take before someone realizes that J.F.K. are your initials too?"

"Meaning they already have?"

"Father Dowling has. He wants to see you."

"What for?"

"Jack, you are going to need all the help you can get. You realize that, don't you? It was a cruel thing to try to make me think your father had done this."

"You're a fine one to talk about cruelty. I didn't do this to hurt him."

"You're the one who's going to be hurt. They will do the same thing at that motel they did with your father."

"Did you give that priest a picture of me?"

"No."

Their eyes were drawn simultaneously to the table beside the couch. It was one of those times when what is absent is more visible than what is present. The photograph of Jack, Junior was no longer there.

26

WHEN THE reporter Mervel showed her the old newspaper photograph and asked her if this was the guy who had come to see Clare O'Leary, Wilma was almost startled that what she had told Father Dowling should actually be making people like Mervel run all over the place. He told her he had gone up to Milwaukee to check on the man in the picture.

"There's no chance this is the guy?" Mervel looked at Wilma beseechingly.

"No chance in the world. Who is he?"

"It doesn't matter."

He wore the hangdog look of a man who had tried and failed, and not merely failed. She could see he felt foolish too. Well, she knew what that was like. He lit another cigarette and she brought her hand up, prepared to fan away the acrid odor — the smell of a just-lighted cigarette was sickening — but she brought the hand to her lips instead.

"I'm sorry."

"It's not your fault."

Mervel's complexion looked as if it had been dyed by cigarette smoke. As for his body, forget it. How could anyone let himself go so completely? Smoking, drinking, no exercise, he was making himself a candidate for a heart attack. She told him so.

"You want me to take up weightlifting or something?"

"You should run."

"Jog?" He showed his yellow teeth in a smile. "You're kidding. People see me puffing down the street, they'd throw a net over me."

"Who's going to see you? Is that it, are you proud?"

She kept after him a bit, it was her job, and she did like him, sort of, attracted by the woebegone air. Why did she always fall for losers? Had Twinkie been a loser? Of course he had. He might have looked in better shape than Mervel, in some ways he was, but he abused his body just as much, maybe more. She doubted that Mervel could afford coke. Before he left, she asked to see the picture again, so he wouldn't think he had completely wasted his time. But she didn't want to give him false hope either. The man in the picture was twice as old as J.F.K. In a way, she felt as disappointed as Mervel.

Would they keep on looking for J.F.K.? Wilma doubted it after Mervel told her who the man in the picture was. That would have been a connection, all right, though just how she didn't see. Neither did Mervel.

"Anyway, there isn't a connection, so that's it. How about coming downstairs and having a drink with me?"

He must have meant the Billet-Doux. She couldn't have gone there, even if she did drink; the memories of Twinkie would have been too much, and it would have been hard to ignore what a comedown from Twinkie Mervel was. Not that there had ever been anything with Twinkie, really, but Wilma was sure there would have been, if Twinkie had lived. She and Mervel went up the street to a fast-food place where Wilma ordered a salad and a glass of milk. Mervel had their biggest hamburger and a malted. It figured.

Back at the Inn, Ganser phoned up to tell her she had a visitor. "A priest," he explained, and he might have been announcing a man from Mars.

"I'll come down."

"He'll be waiting in the lobby. A priest."

Ganser obviously preferred having Dowling sitting in the lobby rather than in his office. No wonder, given some of the pictures he had on the walls in there, to say nothing of the lingering aroma of pot.

Father Dowling was not seated and he came toward her as soon as she emerged from the elevator.

"I offered to go up. He seemed to think I would lose my way. The manager."

"It's just a gym. Would you like to see it?"

"You're probably busy."

"No. Come on up."

There was an overweight salesman broiling in the sauna, getting ready to overeat tonight. She took Roger Dowling into her office, after giving him a quick tour of the premises. He shook his head.

"Motels offer every convenience nowadays, don't they?"

In the office, he took a framed picture from the sack he carried and handed it to her. And there, smiling up at her, looking innocent as a choirboy, was J.F.K.

"That's him."

"You're sure?"

He did not appear happy that she had recognized the man in the photograph. The priest looked as if he had gotten bad news rather than good.

He said, "This young fellow came here to meet Mrs. O'Leary?"

"That's right."

He got out a pipe and began to fumble with it. "They had dinner together, that sort of thing?"

Wilma turned in her swivel chair and looked out the window. Through its sooty panes she was given an impressionistic view of the Fox River skyline. She had a very vivid image of the young man in the photograph standing at Mrs. O'Leary's door. Wilma had been giving a massage to a woman whose room was on that corridor and saw the door open and the young man go right in. It was one of those moments when all sorts of things seemed to fall in place. The young man entering the room solved the mystery of Mrs. O'Leary, a mystery Wilma had some interest in because she did not quite believe Twinkie when he laughed off the suggestion that he had something going with the O'Leary woman. Well, she had been right the first time.

"There is certainly the factual correlation of their stays here." Suddenly he laughed. "Good Lord, I am beginning to sound like a machine."

"Who is he?"

"You haven't any idea?"

"Don't tell me his name is really Kinton."

"He is the son of the man whose picture Mervel showed you."

"I don't get it."

He smiled sadly. "Neither do I."

"Do the police know?"

He shook his head.

"You'll have to tell them, won't you?"

He looked as if she had caused him physical pain. "Oh, they'll learn of it soon enough. Others here should be able to identify this picture, shouldn't they? I mean, there's no need to put the burden on you."

"People here aren't all that anxious to help the police. Neither am I, for that matter. But it's thinking about Twinkie makes me want someone to pay for it. I know he didn't put all those bullets into Twinkie." She nodded at the photograph he had put back into the sack. "But he is connected with it somehow. It wouldn't have happened if it hadn't been for him. So he shouldn't just walk away from it all, should he?"

"Nobody really does walk away from what he's done." He smiled. "Now I sound like a sermon machine."

She went down in the elevator with him. Why not? A little courtesy to the clergy did no harm. Besides, Twinkie had been Catholic and she felt he would appreciate her being nice to Father Dowling.

She stood in the little area between the two sets of glass doors and watched him go out to his car. Priests mystified her. She could not figure out what makes them tick. Father Dowling got into his car, eased it out of its spot, and drove slowly past the entrance. The priest was unaware of Wilma standing there watching him go.

And then she saw J.F.K. He was in a car that went by after the priest's. Without thinking, Wilma pushed her way outside. The priest had turned right into the street and the car with J.F.K. at the wheel turned right too.

Wilma had no doubt J.F.K. was following the priest.

27

KNOWING Dave Hogan as well as he did, it was hard for Larry O'Leary not to think how much better a priest he would have made than his friend. Hogan's behavior since Clare's body had been found was meant to be helpful, Larry would grant him that. But the fact was, Hogan hadn't been a damned bit of real help.

Just from the side of consolation alone, if a priest wasn't good in that department, what good was he? Couldn't he at least imagine what it was like for him, losing a wife like Clare? Clare was his connection with the past, when he had been a better man than he was today, an admission he had not made quite so baldly to Hogan, but it was there to be seen if someone had the eyes to see. Of course Hogan didn't know about Andrea.

He really didn't. For a while Larry thought the priest was just being discreet. See no evil, that sort of thing. But the truth was, he didn't have a clue. Maybe Larry O'Leary would have made a good priest, but he wasn't one. Andrea was attractive, not least because she did not spell Danger. Most women spelled Danger. If they didn't, a man in Larry O'Leary's position could have been in bed the better part of his life. As Clare thought he was. But it was worth his ears to sport with every Amaryllis in the shade: they were too young, or they had husbands, or they had long-term designs on his freedom. There was almost always something, the more so when this was denied. Larry O'Leary was never more skeptical than when confronted with a woman who claimed that all she wanted was a quickie, wham-bang and that's all, good friends after or forget all about it, that was up to him.

It is not in woman's nature to take such a straightforwardly selfish approach to matters of the flesh. Promiscuity is a male vice, no doubt about it. So then what about Andrea?

The big difference here was that she was his lawyer. A good solid business relationship sustained any monkey business they might engage in. He could feel he was doing her a favor; she could tell herself she was just cementing relations with a client. Plus, she was a feminist. There is no better target of opportunity for the male chauvinist than a liberated woman. To Larry O'Leary it was as plain as the nose on your face that women's liberation was a cunning plot hatched by people like Hefner. Andrea was a classic case. She could interpret her availability for him as independence on her part. Wonderful. Plus, she was an older woman.

Older women are better. There are many reasons for this, but the fact is not in doubt. Andrea was very good indeed. In fact, so good she made Larry feel, well, everything he liked to be with a woman.

But the present point of all this is that the Reverend David Hogan had no idea it was going on. He had actually been shocked when Clare had gone to him with her story. Larry O'Leary unfaithful? The priest seemed to think this was tantamount to recanting the faith. Larry half suspected Dave was putting him on, that there was something of the put-down in his incredulity. But, to give him credit, he had the parallel business of the joke about putting out a contract on Clare to go by. If that was silly, so was the claim that Larry was playing around.

Even if Hogan had been a wizard up till now, he was useless when Andrea broke the news of her son's involvement in the Fox River events.

"Who knows besides you?" Hogan asked, whispering.

"Dave," Larry said, "everyone is going to know."

"Father Dowling knows," Andrea said.

Hogan clapped his bald head and let out a groan. "Oh, no. Dowling."

"He told me, Father."

"You mean he was guessing. That's his way. He guesses this and guesses that and people play his game and..."

"Dave," O'Leary said in disgust, "either the kid's involved or he's not involved. It's got nothing to do with Dowling or who knows it or any other goddamn thing."

Larry wished Dowling were here now. Well, not exactly here. With Hogan and Andrea, his office at the station was already pretty crowded. He went around his desk and crouched in front of Andrea.

"Dowling came to your house and told you a reporter had the bright idea that your husband had been the J.F.K. who was at the Stagecoach Inn every time Clare was. He gets a picture and draws a blank. Then is it Dowling or the reporter who thinks of your son?"

"Not the reporter. Father Dowling."

"So why does he drive all the way to Waukegan to tell you. He can't telephone?"

Andrea had achieved a condition of icy calm. She followed what he said as if he were reciting a lesson and she would be the judge of whether or not he got it right. "Because he wanted a photograph of Jack, Junior."

"Did you give him one?"

"He took one."

"He stole it? He stole a photograph from your house!" Hogan's voice sounded strangled. It was easier to ignore the priest when you got him behind your back.

"Took a picture and left. And then Jack, Junior shows up. How much later?"

"Maybe ten minutes. It wasn't a long time after Father Dowling had gone."

"How long did your son stay?"

"Again, not very long."

"Where did he say he was going?"

"He didn't. Larry, he was going to follow Roger Dowling. I'm as sure of that as I'm sitting here. That is why I'm sitting here. Call it a reversal of roles. I want advice. What am I going to do?"

"Nothing!" Hogan cried. "Do nothing. Larry has just gotten out of this mess and we don't want him back in it."

"Dave, do me a favor, will you? Shut up."

When you stop to think of it, who's going to tell a priest to shut up? His housekeeper? Forget it. Without a wife, he probably thinks that his assessment of how he's doing is the public one. In any case, it was clear from the expression on Dave Hogan's face that he had not been told to shut up for a very long time. Larry turned back to Andrea.

"You are going to call the Fox River police. Maybe they've already made the link between Jack, Junior and those names in the Stagecoach register. Maybe they haven't. They have to know."

"Won't Roger Dowling tell them?"

Larry looked over his shoulder. Hogan sat there with his mouth hung open in shock. "What do you think, Father? Would Dowling go to the police?"

Hogan's egg-shaped head went back and forth. "I don't think so."

"Why not?"

"A priest doesn't want to be the one who brings someone to justice. Besides, he'll figure it's only a matter of time."

"And he'd be right."

Larry went back to the desk, picked up the phone, and dialed 9 for an outside line. He didn't want his secretary putting through a call to the Fox River police. While he waited for the call to go through, he put his hand over the receiver and said to Andrea, "Then we ought to go over there. Don't you think?"

"Good idea," said the recovered Dave Hogan.

28

THE CALL was put through to Keegan and, even though it was Larry O'Leary on the phone, a man with whom he had felt a fleeting sense of identity, the Captain of Detectives was not disposed to be credulous.

"J.F.K.," he repeated, and it was like recalling a practical joke of which he had been the victim. "Yes, I remember. The man named Kinton who stayed at the Stagecoach."

"I believe it was your men who established there is no J. F. Kinton." O'Leary sounded as though he were reading a script.

"We found that there is no one of that name living at the address given by whoever registered." Keegan was trying to be careful, but he knew he sounded mealy-mouthed. It was the sort of restriction on what you can say in court that he felt in the grips of now. The less he claimed for the investigation into the death of Clare O'Leary, not to mention those of Hilda and Zeugner, the less inadequate he felt.

"You will have noticed, I am sure, that those initials fit the former husband of my lawyer Andrea Kohler as well. Needless to say, Ms. Kohler was not disposed to be helpful when Mervel of the Fox River *Messenger* came over here. It looked like a wild-goose chase."

"What the hell are you getting at, O'Leary?"

"You do know of Mervel's visit, don't you?"

"I'm asking what you are getting at, not what some goddamn reporter is up to."

"Well, when he drew a blank with the photograph, he apparently let it go. But Father Dowling saw the further suggestion."

Keegan was punching the buttons attached to his phone, signaling to get Cy or Lamb or somebody in here while he tried to carry on this infuriating conversation. What in the hell had Mervel been up to? Worse, what was his supposed friend Roger Dowling doing in Waukegan and God knew where else without letting either the Fox River police or Phil Keegan know? Larry O'Leary seemed incapable of uttering a straight sentence.

"I don't know of any photograph," Keegan shouted.

Cy looked in the door, his brows raised in a question, and Keegan beckoned him in with a savage movement of his arm. He said, without covering the receiver, "Pick up the other phone."

"That's Andrea Kohler on the other phone, Captain. She wanted to listen in."

"I want you to promise to arrest him, not harm him," Andrea Kohler said, sobbing.

Keegan, fighting for patience, said, "Look. I am going to put Lieutenant Horvath on. Tell him everything and start at the beginning, for the love of God. Pretend he doesn't even know why you called."

When Cy had it, Keegan punched a button for an outside line and dialed the number of St. Hilary's. While he was waiting, Agnes Lamb came in.

"Did you want me, Captain?"

"Listen in on that call Cy is taking. Have you seen Mervel lately?"

"The reporter? No."

Marie Murkin answered the phone, her voice as always frosty and efficient. It melted when she recognized Keegan.

"Is Father Dowling there, Marie?"

"He has someone with him, Captain. I can disturb him if you like."

No, Phil Keegan thought. I'll disturb him myself. To Marie he merely offered his thanks and hung up. He caught Horvath's eye and whispered Dowling's name. Cy nodded. Then Keegan was pounding down the hall. His main thought was still that Roger Dowling had betrayed him, he didn't quite know how.

He came up out of the garage faster than he should have and as soon as he hit the street he flicked on the siren. If nothing else, it vented some of the frustration he felt. It was bad enough running into brick walls trying to figure out the cause of three dead bodies in his jurisdiction; it was bad enough that Robertson and the politicians seemed determined to thwart police efforts to see that justice was done. Now he had all kinds of free-lance stuff going on, local journalists raising hell in Waukegan about Fox River murders, and, the most unkindest cut of all, as the priest would have put it, Roger Dowling apparently knowing a lot more than he was telling.

That had been the story since the beginning of this case. Roger had not been forthcoming about Clare O'Leary's visit to him shortly before she was found dead in her room at the Stagecoach Inn. There might have been reasons for that, confidential, penitent and priest, that sort of thing, but that did not cover trips to Waukegan and what was pretty obviously an independent investigation of a pending case. If this were someone other than Roger Dowling, there was no doubt what would be done about it. At the moment Phil Keegan was not about to consider the pastor of St. Hilary's an exception.

He switched off the siren when he left the Crosstown; he came down the ramp too fast and the car went into a skid when he applied the brakes. He came to a stop at an angle without sliding into traffic and he sat there for a moment trying to let the vexation and anger drain from him. But as he eased into the traffic, resisting the impulse to clear the way with the siren, he felt his anger mount again. As a result, when he pulled up in front of the rectory he really needed the brakes, and there was a protest of rubber as the tires scraped along the curb. Keegan hopped out quickly and hurried toward the house. He was not so disturbed that he did not notice the car parked in front of the church.

There was no answer to his first push on the bell, nor to his second. Go around to the kitchen? He knew Marie Murkin was in the kitchen. But if he knew that, he also knew Roger Dowling was home. He pulled open the outer door and grabbed the handle of the frame door. The pressure of his thumb, a forward push, and the door eased open. Phil Keegan put his head in first.

The door of the study was open and the light coming from it illumined the body of Marie Murkin.

The housekeeper lay crumpled against a wall of the hallway, one arm thrown up and over her head, the other clutching at her throat. Keegan was inside and crouching beside her in a single movement. He could have cried out in relief when he heard her breathing escaping her like a slight moan.

On his feet again, gun in hand, Keegan went to the door of the study and called out, "Roger?"

How oddly unauthoritative his voice sounded. But just a moment before he had thought he was looking at the dead body of Marie Murkin. He took his gun off safety, then rounded the door in a single movement, arms out from his body, ready for anything. But there was only the empty study. Empty except for the heavy clouds of pipe smoke still hanging in the air. Roger could not have been gone for more than a minute or two.

Keegan pocketed his weapon and went back to Marie Murkin. Her eyes opened, focused, saw him, and then she screamed, screamed and scrambled to embrace his legs like an inept tackler. Great sobs broke from her as she more or less coherently thanked God.

He got free of her by crouching once more and helping her get propped in a seated position against the wall.

"Where is he, Marie? Where's Father Dowling?"

"That man . . ." She looked faint again.

"Snap out of it, Marie," he barked. "What man? What are you talking about?"

"He forced him to leave. They heard you drive up. I did too. And I came out of the kitchen and that is when they came out of the study, Father Dowling first, then the man. The man struck me. He pushed me aside. Captain, he was carrying a gun."

"They went through the kitchen?"

Marie nodded wildly. "Yes, yes."

Phil Keegan stepped around her and into the kitchen. The back door was ajar. From it, access was gained to a small porch and to the walkway that led across the lawn to the side door of the church. Remembering the car parked in front of the church, Phil Keegan took the walkway to the street. Running. His gun in his hand again.

29

AFTER seeing that the man who had called himself Kinton was indeed following Father Dowling, Wilma ran back into the motel, unsure what she should do. Call the police? But what could she tell them that made any sense? Ganser stood behind the check-out desk. Briefly, Wilma considered asking the manager what she should do. But that was as silly as wishing Twinkie were still here so she could enlist his help. She hurried across the lobby to the pay phones.

As she flipped through the pages of the telephone directory, she could have kicked herself for not having written down the address the first time she had looked it up. Clare O'Leary had had sense enough to do that.

Two minutes later she was running out to her car. She had not told Ganser she was going; she remembered the fat salesman who was still trying to work off a few pounds in her gym. But she simply did not have time to go up there if she was going to be of any help to Father Dowling.

Although she had lived there now for months and months, Wilma did not know Fox River very well. Any time off she had, she headed for the Loop or Old Town or Water Tower Place. The thought of shopping or having any fun in Fox River just never occurred to her. The fact that she had been there before did not help; she had trouble finding the church and rectory.

She knew she was there when she saw the car that had followed Father Dowling parked in front of the church. Wilma circled the parish plant and put her own car among those in the lot behind the school. And then she headed for the church.

The front door was huge, and she made a little bet with herself that it would be locked. She lost, but it took her several hefty pulls to realize it. And then she went inside.

Wilma's idea of church was of a white frame building with clear panes of glass in the windows so that the interior was exactly as bright as outside. Without people in it a church in her sense was less than a place. But St. Hilary's, cool and dark and gloomy, was like a church in a movie. She stopped when she came into the nave and put out her hand. She drew it back immediately. Water? There was water in a sort of carved-out stone pillar behind the back pew. Strange. As strange as the smells of the place and the patches of color that lay all about after riding rays of sun down from the stained-glass windows.

Wilma stood as still as she could and listened. She thought she might hear voices, but the only sounds were the creaking of boards and the low hum of a fan high in the walls. Her eyes drawn upward, Wilma looked at the great light fixtures suspended from chains from the ceiling. Not all the light came from the windows. In an alcove toward the front of the church a cheerful multicolored light was visible. Wilma stretched to the right and saw the banks of vigil lights.

Strange as she found the church, she could sense the peace it conveyed to others. And it was that peace which was endangered by the man who had followed the priest home. That was his car out front, she was sure of it. So he must be in the church.

After she was used to the place a bit, she could see there was no one else in sight. She started slowly up the aisle, toward the main altar. Through the portion of the window that was tipped open sounds came from outside. She found them reassuring. There was a familiar world she could go back into after she had made sure Father Dowling was not in danger.

Where was he? As she neared the altar she could see there

was a large room off to the left of it, but strain as she might she still could not pick up the sound of voices. Turning, she started back. Along the sides of the church there were closed doors, three in a row, an interval, then three more. Suddenly she guessed what they were. Confessionals! It was where people went to tell their sins to the priest. She had heard about that and Twinkie had assured her it was true, and there they were. She felt a not unpleasant shiver pass over her.

Is that where the priest and his pursuer had ended up? The thought made Wilma want to break into a run. But then she heard voices and turned. They came from the front of the church. She froze, half expecting the two men to appear. They did not, though the voices continued to be audible.

Her heart in her throat, Wilma worked her way through a pew to the side aisle and began to move once more toward the front of the church. When she came to the alcove where all the little candles were alight, she saw the statue of the mother of Jesus. For the first time in her life Wilma asked Mary to intercede for her. One of the voices she could hear now was that of Father Dowling.

Her guess was that they were in the room off the altar. The other voice was angry and excited and contrasted dramatically with the measured calm of the priest's voice. It seemed pretty clear that the priest was trying to stop the man from panicking.

Wilma stepped into the alcove and picked up one of the waxen tapers and touched it into light from the flame of a burning candle. She lit a candle of her own and it seemed exactly the right thing to do in the circumstances. Don't let anything happen to him, she murmured. There have been too many deaths already.

Not wholly dissatisfied with her prayer, Wilma stepped back. And that is when she tipped over the large glass-enclosed three-day candle. It broke with an enormous bang and the scattering shards of glass filled the church with their tinkling notes.

30

"I BELIEVE you're looking for me, Father."

John F. Kohler, Jr. was sufficiently like the photograph Roger Dowling had borrowed from his mother's living room to make the recognition easy. What was not easy was to understand how the young man knew Roger Dowling had connected him with the Stagecoach Inn.

"My mother told me, Father."

His courtesy might have been mockery, but the deference in his voice seemed genuine.

"Come in."

Marie Murkin had not heard the bell and Father Dowling had gone to the front door himself. Marie was in the doorway of the kitchen when the pastor and his visitor came down the hallway to the study. Young Kohler bowed in her direction and then waited for Father Dowling to precede him into the study. Seated, he refused coffee, said he did not smoke, gave a dismissive laugh when asked if he minded pipe smoke.

"I've often wished I could acquire the taste myself, Father."

"Now, what did your mother tell you?"

"I have come here to speak to you as a priest, Father."

"I'm glad to hear that."

"I mean that I wish what I say to be between you and me."

"You want to make your confession?"

"Father, I have committed murder."

"How many times?"

Kohler ignored the question. "I killed Clare O'Leary."

"Why?"

"It would be easier if I knew how much you know, Father Dowling. Do you know of her husband, the radio announcer?"

"Larry O'Leary? Yes."

"Often on the air he spoke of his efforts to have his wife killed. By a hired assassin."

"Surely you can't pick up WKIS in Florida?"

"I have been north frequently during this past year. We have submitted a number of bids in the Chicago and Milwaukee areas, successfully several times. My father could not bear to see Milwaukee again, so it fell to me to come here and to get under way the projects we had succeeded in landing. My mother's connection with O'Leary made me curious. His remarks about his wife seemed in the worst of taste. I resolved to find out what she was like."

"What was she like?"

"She deserved to die. She was a hypocrite. She led a double life. You will say that it is not up to me to decide who deserves to live or die. I agree. I myself no longer deserve to live, after what I have done. But I want to go on living. That is why I do not propose to be caught."

"Tell me about killing her."

"We had a very interesting conversation, first in the lounge, later in her room. She had been to talk to a priest, she said. She was ashamed of the way she lived, the way her husband lived, the way my mother lived. I think she was genuinely sorry. That gives me comfort, Father. While that did not exculpate her, there is a good chance she was repentant when she died."

"Her death was considered a suicide."

"At first. That did not upset me. I knew the truth of the matter. Besides, I had arranged things in such a way that suicide would seem the obvious explanation. Until the autopsy. I was appalled when the drugs were not found in the autopsy. I knew she had been taking them regularly."

"You gave her the sleeping pills?"

"Dissolved in a drink. A dozen and a half of them. After she became drowsy, I put a pillow over her face and held it there until she stopped breathing. I was very gentle. I imagined her soul going to God."

"Did you ever talk to the man who entertained in the lounge? Twinkie Zeugner?"

"No."

"He was killed, shot down."

"That is not my fault."

"You didn't kill him?"

"Why would I want to do that!" The young man seemed almost shocked.

"I still do not understand why you wanted to kill Clare O'Leary."

"There were several reasons. The life she lived was one. Her husband's silly talk about her on the radio. And my mother. It seemed a way of getting at her. If O'Leary were blamed for his wife's death, as he should be, if he were convicted, he would be put away and..."

Kohler spoke in the most matter-of-fact tones, however outrageous what he was saying. Seldom had Roger Dowling listened to so reasonable a voice. The young man professed to be sorry for what he had done, but his voice sounded no different when he said that than when he described in more detail how he had administered the sleeping pills to Clare O'Leary. His visit to Roger Dowling shared in the logic of his life.

"Will you give me absolution, Father?"

"It's not quite that simple in the circumstances."

"You cannot tell anyone what I have said to you."

"That's right."

Kohler had sat forward, his first show of emotion. Now he sat back, apparently relieved.

"That does not mean you're safe. I am not the only one who had connected you with the Stagecoach Inn and Clare O'Leary."

He smiled. "My mother is unlikely to turn me in."

"There are others."

He shook his head. "Don't, Father. I know that isn't true. I'd like the photograph you took from my mother."

It was when Roger Dowling opened his desk drawer to get the photograph that there was the sound of a car braking outside. Kohler was on his feet immediately. He came swiftly around the desk and took Roger Dowling's arm as he looked out the window. And then he was propelling the priest out of the study.

In the hallway they encountered Marie Murkin. Kohler swept her aside and forced Roger Dowling into a trot as they crossed the kitchen. They were in full flight when they went along the sidewalk to the side door of the church.

"Who is he?" Kohler asked when they came to a halt in the sacristy.

"He is a policeman. Captain Keegan."

"How did he know I was here?" Kohler at first seemed to see this as merely a conceptual puzzle. But his grip on Roger Dowling's arm grew tighter and together they paced the sacristy.

"I told you that others would suspect you."

"I used to be an altar boy, Father. My mother helped me memorize the Latin responses. You don't use Latin anymore, do you? So much has changed. Like my mother. She wanted to be her own woman. That meant she did not want to be my mother anymore. I can't stop being her son. How can she stop being my mother? I couldn't kill *her*."

"Why don't we go talk to Captain Keegan?"

The façade of calm reasonableness went completely.

"No! I am leaving. And you are going to help me. My car is parked outside the front of the church. You will leave by the side door, the door we entered, and divert the policeman. Retain him. I don't care how. Promise me you won't tell him I was here."

"I am afraid he already knows."

"He can't!"

"Where will you go?"

"I have projects to look after." He actually glanced at his watch. "Come, let's go."

They had left the sacristy and were in a small areaway from which a door opened into the nave of the church when the sound of breaking glass stopped them. There was no doubt it had come from the body of the church. That left only the side door.

Still gripping Roger Dowling's arm, Kohler skipped down the three steps to the side door and pushed it open. They came running into the sunny day and for a moment Roger Dowling could not see. But he heard the sound of Kohler's breath escaping and felt his fingers loosen and then drop away.

It took the priest a moment to regain his balance and his sight. He brought his hand to his brow, to shut out the sun. Kohler lay face down on the lawn, one hand pulled up behind him. Phil Keegan, his knee planted in Kohler's back, his hand exerting pressure on the fallen young man's arm, looked up at Roger Dowling.

"No need to salute, Roger."

"I was going to ask you not to genuflect."

Along the sidewalk from the rectory, hands fluttering, arms outstretched, her eyes rolling in excitement, came Marie Murkin.

"Thank God you caught him," she cried. "Thank God you caught him."

And she bustled right by the pastor, took Phil Keegan's head between her two hands, and kissed him soundly on the forehead.

They turned when the church door opened again and Wilma stepped into the sunlight. Her eyes focused on Father Dowling and she looked apologetic.

"I broke something in there," she said. "A candle. I'll pay for it."

And then her expression changed as she became aware of the

scene there on the walk. Captain Keegan holding J.F.K. to the ground, the housekeeper hovering over him like an affectionate referee at a wrestling match. Father Dowling told Wilma it didn't matter. Everything was all right.

Except for the fact that not every misdeed could be made up for so easily as a broken candle. But sorrow, even as a form of politeness, is a beginning. He hoped young Kohler's desire to confess was as genuine as Wilma's.

31

IT WAS unwise, Father Dowling discovered, to mention Mrs. Murkin's display of affection there on the sidewalk either to the housekeeper or to Phil Keegan. Mrs. Murkin narrowed her eyes and made a line of her lips and maintained a Trappistine silence, refusing to be jollied about it. Keegan tried to joke it away and that only made it worse.

"Housekeepers go for me," he growled. Mrs. Murkin took away the bottle beside his chair, although it was still half full of beer.

"Thomas More married again," Roger Dowling murmured, fussing over his pipe.

"And they killed him," Phil Keegan said.

There was a sound of supreme impatience from the kitchen.

"So what about Zeugner and Hilda?" the pastor of St. Hilary asked.

"She took away my beer."

"Get another."

Keegan hesitated, then went reluctantly into the kitchen. Roger Dowling listened but no words were exchanged. Maybe Phil would welcome Marie Murkin's silent treatment.

Returned, sipping his beer, Keegan frowned. "It looks like young Kohler couldn't have done them. Certainly not the Zeugner killing. That was a mob action if ever there was one."

"Maxwell?"

"We can't place him in the High-Rise."

"He was there."

"I need more than your word for it. Oh, we have some evidence. But Robertson won't hear of it."

"And Hilda?"

Keegan shrugged. "Either way. If she saw Kohler, the kid would have had a motive. It might have had something to do with Zeugner. We don't know."

Roger Dowling did not envy Phil the task of persuading Agnes Lamb that the slaying of Hilda and Zeugner, like that of Harley, must be consigned to the unsolved crime file. If Phil had free rein, he would pursue those killings with more tenacity than Agnes. It did not sit well with the Captain of Detectives that there should be injustices unpunished in his jurisdiction. Well, it was unrealistic to expect police to adopt a priest's view of the matter. Roger Dowling could live with the thought of unpunished crimes so long as there was the hope that sins should be forgiven.

"How is Agnes Lamb reacting to all this?"

Phil groaned. "I suggested she should run for mayor and appoint a chief who would back me up."

"That's not a bad idea."

"Cy called it a racist suggestion."

"What did Agnes say?"

"I think she likes the idea."

It was hard to tell whether Phil himself did. Not that he wouldn't like a chief other than Robertson.

Kohler's lawyer was working on an insanity plea. The lawyer's name was Yolton and he had visited the rectory to elicit from Roger Dowling testimony to his client's defective mental health. The priest disclaimed awareness of it.

"Father, he killed a woman in cold blood."

"Yes."

"Isn't that crazy?"

The priest smiled. "It's certainly wrong."

When he himself talked with Kohler he had difficulty making the young man see the enormity of what he had done.

"Yolton says he can get me off."

"That's not what I meant."

Kohler looked at him. "Oh. Sure. I've been to confession. The chaplain here gave me absolution."

Roger Dowling would have liked to feel more pleased than he did. Does anyone see his own deeds with clarity? It was hard to think that Kohler saw the true import of what he had done. His father did.

Kohler, Senior had a smooth boyish face under a thatch of gray hair but there was a pain deep in his eyes that had no remedy this side of the grave. He had lost his wife, now he had lost his son.

"I blame myself, Father Dowling. Where the hell did I go wrong?"

"It's not that simple," Roger Dowling said.

Mr. Kohler was not convinced. Perhaps he needed to feel responsible for his whole family. His daughters refused to believe their brother had killed anyone. They had heard stories about the Chicago suburbs. It was the mob, they were sure of it. It looked as if they were two-thirds right.

"It's a messy ending," Phil Keegan groused.

"Isn't it always?"

"No!"

But even on Phil's terms, law and punishment, endings were often messy. Roger Dowling thought beyond that, to mercy and redemption, the ultimate sorting out. He began a special commemoration in his Mass for the soul of Twinkie Zeugner.

Such a life, playing piano in the semi-dark to the half-drunk, night after night, enslaved to drugs. Perhaps any life can be made to seem absurd. But each of us gets only one, and one is enough to work out our destiny. Improbable as it might sound, it was conceivable that Twinkie Zeugner, with his residual faith and self-knowledge, had crooned his way into heaven in the smoky atmosphere of the Billet-Doux. But that was a thought he did not wish to develop for Phil Keegan's edification.

"He would have made a good cop," Phil said. "He had the build for it."

"Does anyone want popcorn?" Marie Murkin's propitiatory question drifted in from the kitchen.

Phil Keegan wanted popcorn. Roger Dowling said he would have some too. Keegan went into the kitchen to help, and for a moment the priest stared at the chair he had vacated and thought of Mrs. O'Leary sitting there, telling him she had left her husband. Larry O'Leary planned to remarry, now that he was free, choosing to ignore the fact that his lawyer was not so disencumbered. Somehow Roger Dowling thought Clare O'Leary was freer than either of them.